The Year of the Tiger

The Year
of
the Tiger

Phineas Cricket

Cosmic Turtle Books

Published by Cosmic Turtle Books, 2025

www.cosmicturtlebooks.com

ISBN: 979-8-9911550-7-6

Cover design by Tim Barber

A Note to the Reader

Some of the characters in this story speak Singlish, an informal variety of English spoken in Singapore. For help with specific words and phrases, see the glossary at the back of this book.

Singapore, 1974

Chapter 1

Today, like every day, Mike paused to check the mail table on his way up to the dorm. There was still a big enough stack of letters to sort through, so he took his time studying every postage stamp, savoring the handwriting on each envelope, checking the name of the kid it was addressed to. As if by drawing out time he could draw out hope, and for those few minutes everything was normal, and maybe the next envelope in the pile would bear his own name, in the familiar cursive writing of his mother's hand.

"Mrs. Watkins, Mike's doing it again!" said Ming, punching his shoulder. "He's hogging the mail!"

Mike frowned at her, resisting the urge to punch her back. "I am *not*," he said.

Mrs. Watkins' sandals came flicking in from the assembly room, and Mike steeled himself for a scolding. But she didn't look mad when she appeared—old-lady eyes smiling tenderly from nests of wrinkles, behind a cage of wire-framed glasses. "Mike, it's almost dinner time. Didn't I ask you to put a shirt on?"

"I was just going," said Mike. He looked dagger-eyes at Ming as he turned toward the stairs.

Mrs. Watkins called him back. "Wait, Mike. Come inside. I've been meaning to talk to you."

Inside. The Inner Sanctum. Mrs. Watkins' private bedroom with its own personal bathroom attached. Unlike most other rooms at the Christian Children's Hostel, Mrs. Watkins' room had a home-like feel, with family pictures and knickknacks and warm lighting.

Mike sensed that he was in some kind of trouble. He felt the cool air from the ceiling fan on his naked shoulders and wished he had put

1

a shirt on like he'd been told. But he followed her obediently into the room and sat stiffly in an upholstered armchair. Mrs. Watkins perched on the edge of her bed and looked at him.

"Mike, I got another call from your grandmother today."

He stared, feeling the blood drain from his face.

"They would love to have you stay with them, until things get sorted out. We all know this has been a hard time for you. Being with family might—"

"No," said Mike. The brusqueness of his voice made Mrs. Watkins frown. He added more softly: "Please."

"Oh, Mike. It's been more than six weeks."

Mrs. Watkins gave him that *understanding* look that made him feel like a hopeless case. Which he probably was. But he also had a promise to keep, and faith the size of a mustard seed to make it true.

"I can't just leave them there."

Mrs. Watkins sighed through her nose, tight-lipped, as if there were words trapped inside that she dared not say. "Of course. You know this is your home for as long as you need it to be."

Mike nodded, looking down at his sneakers, which were blurring into watery smudges.

"Now go put on a shirt, please," said Mrs. Watkins.

He stood and marched stiffly out of the room, leaving the door open behind him. When he got to the stairs, he ran.

Mike knew something was fishy when he found both roommates sitting on their beds with books open, pretending to read. Bryan wore his usual goofy grin, but Krisda was a dead giveaway, keeping his eyes glued to *Lord of the Flies* and snorting as he tried to hold in a lungful of laughs.

"What?" said Mike, stopping halfway across the room.

Then he saw it. Perched atop his mattress, leaning back against the pillow with a Bible opened on its velvet lap. It was Charlie the tiger, resurrected from the dead.

"Dammit! I told you not to—"

He grabbed the stuffed toy by its ear and strode across the room.

The middle dresser drawer was his. He jammed Charlie deep inside it, burying him under socks and underwear. His roommates howled.

"Uh oh, Mikey's mad!"

"Shut up!"

"Oooooh."

He would have to let the teasing run its course, like a passing storm. He dumped himself on his bed and opened up his Bible to hide behind.

It was his mother's fault. She was the one who had insisted on packing him. The tiger had caused a big argument on his last night in Da Nang.

"News flash, Mom. I'm thirteen."

"You never know when you might need an old friend."

He still didn't understand what could have possessed her. She was not normally an insane person. But now Mike and Charlie were stuck with each other. He couldn't just throw the tiger in the garbage or something—it would have felt like an act of murder.

"*God*, Mike. We're only kidding!"

"Damn, man. Grow up a little."

Somewhere in the distance a bell was clanging. Getchu the cook was on the move, swinging her heavy handbell. "Dinner ready. Time for *makan!*"

"Come on, Mike. It's sloppy joes tonight."

Bryan and Krisda were already waiting for him at the door. They always went down together. Passing first through the flimsy screen door at the top of the stairs, descending under the glow of a bare lightbulb teeming with mosquitos, out into the jungly night and back again into the brightness of the dining room, where a gaggle of twenty-six children was gathering. But as soon as Mike got there, Mrs. Watkins wagged her finger at him and sent him back upstairs.

He had forgotten to put on his shirt.

Chapter 2

Mike knew he had seen the man in the Hawaiian shirt before. He just couldn't remember where. One thing was for sure, he didn't look like any kind of Southern Baptist. Most of the other men wore a shirt and tie, and they drove big air-conditioned sedans and brought their wives and children with them. *This* guy rolled up to church in a red Mustang convertible with the top down, and instead of having a family with him, he brought a Lady of the Night.

At least, that's what Bryan said she was.

"What's a Lady of the Night?" asked Mike as they crossed the parking lot to the church.

Bryan rolled his eyes. "*God*, Mike. Have you been living under a rock your whole life?"

Next to the church there was a jungle gym, and the boys climbed up and perched on top. Technically they were too old to climb on monkey bars, but it was a good place to keep watch. From there they had a good view of the man in the Hawaiian shirt, who was opening the passenger door of the Mustang and offering his hand to the Lady, like she was the Queen of England.

"I swear I've seen him somewhere before," said Mike.

But where? There weren't a lot of places Mike ever went, besides school and the hostel. There were rules about where you could go and when. The only exception was Sunday, when you got to choose which church to go to.

The Lady of the Night stepped out of the Mustang in her high heels and miniskirt, hooking a manicured hand around the man's proffered arm. They walked like that across the parking lot, the sky reflected in their sunglasses, like a couple of movie stars.

"Damn," said Bryan. "This I've got to see." He scampered down to the ground, and Mike followed him.

A blast of air conditioning hit Mike as he entered the church, turning his bare arms to gooseflesh. He hurried to catch up to Bryan, but got stuck behind the movie star couple as they promenaded down the aisle. Bryan had already zipped past them to claim the last empty pew. He must not have been betting that the couple would slide themselves in right next to him.

Mike was left standing in the aisle with no place to sit, like the loser in a game of musical chairs. It was getting to that time when everybody was supposed to be quiet and prayerful. The organ was softly playing "Abide with Me," people were bowing their heads.

Then— "Sit down, kid."

It was not so much what he said, but the *way* he said it—not like an adult telling a kid what to do, but more like a guy meeting another guy on equal terms. Not having to smile or say anything phony, because they understood each other.

Mike squeezed himself in next to the man in the Hawaiian shirt, and everybody scooted over a few inches. He wondered if people might mistake them for a family—the mom and dad in the middle, flanked on either side by two sons. The thought gave him a slightly creepy feeling, which he tried to dispel by studying his Bible. But it was hard to focus on the words. The man had muscular arms, tanned and sprinkled with fine blond hairs, and Mike's eyes were drawn to the tattoos. On the man's left forearm, a Chinese dragon snaked out of the sleeve and down toward the wrist. On his other arm, a tattoo tiger prowled.

"Got 'em in Subic Bay when I was in the Navy."

The man's blue eyes were smiling at him. Mike was embarrassed to be caught looking, but the man didn't seem to mind. He turned slightly toward Mike and flexed his right arm. The tiger jumped.

"Woah!" Mike laughed in surprise.

A couple of pews down, an old lady turned in her seat to glare at them. Mike looked away, stifling giggles. The man nudged him gently in the ribs and leaned down, close to his ear. "Been a while since I was in church. I'm relying on you to keep me out of trouble, kid."

Mike looked up and grinned, and after that they didn't say anything. They didn't need to. They just looked at each other now and then like a couple of conspirators.

After the hymn and the Invocation, the boys extricated themselves from the pew to join their youth group gathering at the front. The class left in single file, but Mike, the last one out, stopped at the door to look back.

The man in the Hawaiian shirt lifted a hand to his brow in a casual two-fingered salute. Looking at Mike as if to confirm there was an understanding between them. Mike thought there might be, but he couldn't say what it was.

Chapter 3

After showers, Mike wrapped a sarong around his waist and trekked down the hall. Boys hung out in their rooms or lurked in open doorways in the last half hour before Lights Out, loafing around, telling jokes, writing letters home. Some played chess or checkers or cards, others listened to pirated music on cheap cassette recorders, mouthed the words to songs they knew by heart. "Kung Fu Fighting" was blasting from Bryan's stereo when Mike got back to their room. Krisda danced around, peppering the air with punches and kicks, as he sang along.

"Austin was looking for you," Bryan said. He aimed a nerf ball at the basket across the room and made a perfect shot.

"Hah!" Krisda grunted, pretending to karate-chop Mike in the neck.

"What does Austin want?" said Mike.

Bryan shrugged. "Said he had something to ask you. Said it was none of my business."

Mike tried to remember what he might have done to make Austin mad. But Austin didn't always need a reason, or if he did, he just made one up.

Mike sat at his desk and rummaged in the drawer for his notebook and colored pencils. He had decided it was safest to stay put and work on his comic, since there wasn't much time left before Lights Out. The high school guys had another half hour after that, but even Austin would think twice about bothering them after bedtime.

He opened his notebook and looked at what he had done so far. The Oval Office scene was almost finished, but the boy secret agent looked like a dweeb. That could be funny, but if the dweeb was going to save America, he might need bigger muscles. Or better weapons. Or maybe he could be a cyborg. Mike picked up a pencil and started redrawing the characters, trying to make the boy better looking and the president more like Richard Nixon. He kept working until a shadow fell across the page.

Someone flipped the volume of the stereo down, and Krisda's voice stopped in the middle of his song. Mike felt a waft of warm breath on the back of his neck.

"Are you *avoiding* me?" said Austin.

Mike twisted himself around in his chair to see—the hard jaw, the eyes that were always angry, the muscled body toned from relentless workouts. Austin snatched the notebook off Mike's desk and read the dialogue out loud in a fake high voice. *"Mr. President, we're under attack! We need to activate the cyborg boy immediately!"*

Mike's face burned. He made a grab for the notebook, but Austin lifted it easily out of reach.

"Where were you?" Austin said, tossing the notebook casually into the wastebasket. "I told these losers I was looking for you."

"I was busy." Mike didn't look at the notebook in the trash, and made no move to retrieve it. He kept his eyes squarely on the older boy's hands, which dangled dangerously at his sides.

Austin's upper lip curled. "What are you looking at?"

"Nothing."

Mike glanced at his roommates, only to confirm what he already knew. Bryan and Krisda stood by their beds like petrified rabbits.

"If you're here to beat me up," said Mike, "go ahead. I've got witnesses."

He had said these words straight to Austin's face—but quickly dropped his gaze back to the hands. Tanned on the outside, roughened on the palms from hours of basketball, nails bitten to the quick. The fingers of the right hand twitched, and Mike flinched.

Austin snorted. "I'm not here for *that,* dumbass. I'm here to *invite* you."

Mike guessed it was a joke of some kind. He waited for the punchline.

"Friday after school, some of us are going to the American Club. You want to come?"

Mike heard a gasp from the other side of the room. Krisda and Bryan were gaping at each other like a miracle had just happened. But Mike wasn't fooled.

"Why?" he said, narrowing his eyes. "Why would you want *me* to come?"

"I don't care if you come or not," said Austin. "I'm just giving you a chance. You can bring your idiot roommates if you want."

Normally you had to be in high school to go to the American Club, unless someone invited you. Which *never* happened. For once Krisda and Bryan didn't argue when Austin pulled rank (a rank which technically he did not even have) and ordered them to bed.

"Goodnight, losers." Austin flipped the light switch, and the room went dark. "No talking. I don't want to have to come back and kick your butts." He withdrew into a pie-slice of light from the hall, closing the door after him. For a minute, the only sound was the ceiling fan whirring in the humid dark.

"We could go bowling," said Bryan from across the room.

"And swimming," said Krisda.

"They've got cheeseburgers," said Bryan.

Mike watched the blurry blades of the ceiling fan whirring round and round. He slipped out of his sarong and pulled the sheet up to cover himself.

"*Cheeseburgers*, Mike. Real ones. Not the fake ones Getchu makes."

Mike sighed. "It's got to be a trick."

Across the room, Krisda's eyes shined in the dark. "He won't do anything. We'll be with you."

It seemed the decision was already made. Mike closed his eyes, pulling the sheet down to feel the air cool against his skin, half listening to the excited whispers of his roommates.

Bowling! Swimming! Cheeseburgers!

Sleep came so fast, he barely had time to pray.

Chapter 4

Friday after school they lined up at Mrs. Watkins' desk to collect their allowance. Mrs. Watkins sat upright with her cashbox in front of her, making careful notes in a ledger with a yellow pencil, which now and then she paused to sharpen. The line wriggled with impatience, Bryan and Krisda jumpy like frogs. They had already changed out of their school uniforms into jeans and T-shirts.

"I'll expect you back by 9 o'clock," Mrs. Watkins said as she handed Mike his envelope of cash. You could tell she wasn't happy they were going to the American Club, but there was nothing she could do because they weren't breaking any rules.

They waited for the van to make its last run from the high school. As soon as the old Volkswagen bus came lumbering up the hill, they raced across the yard to meet it.

Austin and Shep were the last to get out. They didn't seem in any hurry as they strolled back toward the dorm.

"Are we going, or not?" said Bryan, following Austin up the stairs.

Austin slammed the screen door in his face.

Bryan came back down, and they waited some more at the outdoor table, counting their money to pass the time. Krisda got bored and went on a reconnaissance mission to see what was going on. When he came back, the impatience was boiling in his voice.

"Man, that Austin making himself pretty like a girl. Brushing his hair fifty times, putting enough of that deodorant crap to make a stink bomb."

A few minutes later the screen door squeaked open again, and they poked their heads around the corner to look. Austin and Shep were coming down the stairs, looking almost like twins in their frayed blue jeans and batik T-shirts and sandals. Austin was petting his perfect hair when he saw the three roommates staring at him. "What?" he said.

At last, they started on their way down the winding road, and Austin went over the "rules."

"Number one. When we get there, stay the hell away from us. Don't talk to us. Don't even *look* at us."

"Number two," added Shep. "Don't embarrass us in front of the babes. Don't do stupid stuff and then pretend to know us."

They caught the bus at Holland Road. It was the beginning of rush hour, so the bus was crowded with sweaty people talking in Hokkien and Malay and Cantonese. A group of schoolboys, still in their uniforms, looked at them suspiciously, then whispered to each other and laughed.

Mike gave up his seat to an old lady and stood in the aisle, bodies pressing against him from every side. Whenever the bus stopped at a traffic light, he sweltered, sprouting beads of sweat that seeped into his clothes. All he could see was people's backs and armpits. If Bryan hadn't grabbed him by the arm and pulled, he would have missed their stop.

"Number three," said Austin as they threaded their way down the crowded sidewalk, sidestepping shoppers and schoolchildren and workers on their way home. "The most important rule of all. Don't tell anyone we're from the hostel. If anything gets back to the old lady, you're *dead*, understand?"

They crossed a street reeking of exhaust fumes and fried noodles. Motorbikes and bicycles and trishaws dodged in and out between stranded cars. Mike had no idea where he was, until he saw the Stars and Stripes rising out of the confusion. The flag hung above the entrance of a modern looking building, which at last he recognized.

Swimming! Bowling! Cheeseburgers!

Austin signed them in at the front door. The security guard eyed them each in turn, before quietly waving them through. Once inside, Shep and Austin headed to the bowling alley, and the three roommates made a beeline for the pool. Seconds later they were in the water.

Bubbles. The shriveling shock of cold. Mike went under into the silence, opening his eyes to the blurry blue. Krisda grabbed at his legs, and they wrestled like eels until their lungs burned, rising together and breaking through. Air never tasted so sweet. Sunlight slanting through trees.

A cannonball contest from the diving board landed them in trouble with the lifeguard. So instead they dived for coins, splashed each other until their eyes stung with chlorine, floated listlessly in imitation of the dead.

Waterlogged, they plopped themselves into rattan chairs at the table they had staked out as home base. A waiter brought them menus and set three glasses on the table.

"How much is a cheeseburger?" asked Bryan.

"Price on menu," said the waiter. "Read the menu can?"

"Six dollars?" said Krisda. "No way, man!"

"Don't want, don't buy," said the waiter, filling their glasses with ice water from a jug. "Set price. Non-negotiable, lah."

"That's like half our allowance," said Bryan. "What a rip-off!"

"It's okay, we can eat when we get home," said Mike. "It's spring rolls tonight."

"I wanted a *cheeseburger!*"

The waiter seemed distracted suddenly. "Accuse me," he said, slipping away into the forest of tables.

"Damn, where he go?" said Krisda.

A minute later the waiter returned. This time he had his notebook open and his ballpoint at the ready. "Three cheeseburgers, is it. Okay, how you want cooked?"

"We *told* you," said Bryan. "We don't have enough money."

"No money, no problem. Club member pay for you."

"Club member?" said Krisda.

The waiter pointed with his chin. "That man got flowers on his shirt one."

At a table across the pool, the sky reflected in his sunglasses, the man in the Hawaiian shirt took a sip of his cocktail. He smiled and touched his forehead in a casual two-fingered salute.

Chapter 5

"What if he's a perv?" said Krisda, pouring ketchup on his fries.

"Who cares?" Bryan picked up his overloaded cheeseburger with both hands. "Anyway, he *can't* be. Look at that babe he's with."

They watched as the Lady of the Night unwrapped herself from the complimentary Club towel she was wearing and bent down to kiss the man on the mouth. They watched her slow bikini-walk to the pool's edge, where she perched, nymph-like, before slipping gracefully into the water.

"Damn," said Krisda.

"The guy's cool, man. With a babe like that—"

"We saw them at church, remember?" said Mike.

"See?" said Bryan, hitting Krisda on the arm. "He goes to church."

By the time they finished their cheeseburgers, the Lady of the Night had finished her swim and laid herself out on a lounge chair to catch the last rays of the sun. The man in the Hawaiian shirt was left alone at his table, chewing leftover ice cubes from his drink. Mike felt sorry for him. But then he saw the wave. A gesture so slight it was almost invisible, like a secret sign.

"Should we go over and say something to him?" asked Mike.

"Like what?" said Bryan, putting on his shirt.

"I don't know, like, 'thanks for the cheeseburgers?'"

"Yeah," said Krisda. "You go, Mike."

"We'll be bowling," said Bryan. "See ya."

Mike stepped tenderly across the hot concrete, his wet swim trunks clinging to his thighs. He saw tiny twins of himself mirrored in the man's sunglasses and felt suddenly self-conscious. But that didn't stop him from doing the right thing. "Thanks for the cheeseburgers, mister," he said.

"Sit down, kid."

Mike looked over his shoulder and felt a pang of regret. Bryan and Krisda were already dressed and heading inside to the bowling alley. "I have to go," he said.

The man glanced across the pool at the disappearing roommates, then looked back at Mike. "I know you were raised better than that." He half smiled as if to show he was only half joking. "Just a minute of your time, okay? Take a seat."

Shamefaced, Mike pulled a chair out and sat down as he'd been told. He couldn't tell if the eyes behind the mirrored lenses were looking at him or not. The silence seemed to last a long time, and he felt a need to fill it with words. "It was really nice of you. The cheeseburgers and all."

The man's right hand fiddled with a small pile of change on the table. He nudged a fifty-cent piece with his forefinger and flicked it into his palm.

"We don't usually get cheeseburgers," Mike continued, watching the coin poke out between the man's fingers, then disappear. "Not real ones. Getchu always puts weird stuff in the meat."

The man turned his hand over, palm down, and the coin danced magically across his knuckles. He said, "It was good to see you in church. You go every Sunday?"

"Um, yessir," said Mike, distracted by the coin trick. "How do you *do* that?"

The man smiled, flipped the coin to Mike. "The name's Jason Keen." He extended his hand across the table, and Mike returned the handshake the way his father had taught him—not squeezing too hard, but not too soft either. "Hi, Mr. Keen. I'm Mike."

He offered the coin back, but Mr. Keen waved it away. "Save it for a soda. You might need one."

"Thanks," said Mike, hoping this was an opening to leave. He stood and looked for a pocket to put the coin in, but couldn't find one.

Mr. Keen gestured at Mike's empty chair, as if to signal they weren't

14

done yet. Mike deflated as he sat back down, clutching the coin in his hand.

"Look, Mike, I know you're a smart kid, so I'm going to be straight with you. Our meeting here isn't exactly a coincidence."

For a second, Mike thought he hadn't heard right. "Excuse me?"

"Your buddy Austin and I bowl sometimes here at the Club. I asked him to do me a favor."

Jason Keen took off his sunglasses. The blue of the eyes was piercing, but Mike tried not to look away.

"So Austin didn't…" Mike realized his jaw was hanging open. He closed his mouth and swallowed. "I don't get it." A tingling sensation was crawling up his spine, and it took him a moment to recognize the feeling for what it was. "I think I'd better go," he said. "My room-mates—"

"Mike—"

The chair made a scraping sound as he stood up. Mike looked wildly around. "Where's my clothes. Who *are* you?"

The man caught Mike's wrist and held it. "I knew your father. We worked together in Nam."

Mike stopped struggling and stared. The grip on his wrist relaxed, and he sat down slowly into his chair, studying Jason Keen's face. "I don't remember you."

Mr. Keen shook his head. "I wouldn't expect you to. I worked in the field a lot."

"My parents. Are they…" His voice sounded cracked.

Mr. Keen's face softened a little. He reached over and touched Mike's shoulder. "Your folks never talked to you much about their work, did they?"

Mike shrugged. "Just that they help people. Stuff like that."

Mr. Keen picked up his cocktail glass, saw that it was empty, put it back. He drummed his fingers on the tabletop, studying Mike carefully from the corners of his eyes. "USAID, Public Safety Division. It's a pretty standard cover."

The tingling between Mike's shoulder blades spread slowly up the nape of his neck. "Wait. You mean they're *spooks?*"

15

Mr. Keen didn't say anything. He put his sunglasses back on. In the mirrored lenses, palm trees beat their heads against the sky.

"Okay, I don't care about that," said Mike quickly. "Just tell me where they are."

Jason Keen sighed, his fingers skimming the table lightly in search of another coin. "I've already told you more than I'm authorized to. Everything is need-to-know, you understand?" He held a 20-cent piece between two fingers and examined it.

"But I *do* need to know!" Mike gripped the edge of the table with both hands. He hadn't realized he was shouting.

Mr. Keen tapped the coin against the tabletop, waiting for Mike to calm down. "I need you to be cool, Mike. Can you handle that?"

Mike tried to blink away the blur in his eyes. He swiped a hand across his face and nodded.

"Maybe we could help each other, Mike. The truth is, your country needs you. But I'm only going to ask this once." He leaned forward, elbows on the table, and spoke almost in a whisper. "Where you live, at the bottom of the hill, there's a hawker who sells soft drinks. You know the one I'm talking about?"

"The soda pop man?"

"Look for me there on your ride back from school. Or not. If you show up, I'll know you're with us. But it's up to you, man." He sat back in his chair. "Now get up and thank me again for the cheeseburgers, and catch up with your friends. They'll be wondering where you are."

Mike got up as he was told. The chair scraped horribly against the concrete floor. His knees were trembling. "Thanks for the cheeseburgers, Mr. Keen," he said.

Chapter 6

"If you tell, I'll beat the crap out of you," said Austin matter-of-factly. He had plonked himself down on the bus seat next to Mike, apparently for the sole purpose of making this announcement.

Mike tried to act cool. "What would I tell? Nothing happened."

The bus was almost empty on the way back. They had room to spread out, and each of the other guys had a whole bus seat of his own. Which just made it weirder that Austin had to sit next to him so close, breathing on him with his stale cheeseburger breath and taking up more than his fair share of seat. It was light inside the bus, and dark outside, so Mike, squashed against the window, could see only their dim reflections in the glass—Mike with his too-big teeth and messed-up hair, Austin looking at him askance like an interrogator who thinks his suspect is lying to him.

"That guy. Did he… touch you?"

Mike shrugged. "Yeah, so?" He was remembering when Jason Keen had touched him on the shoulder and wondering why Austin would even care. He was surprised to see Austin pale a little.

"Where?" said Austin.

"At the swimming pool."

"No, dumbass. I mean where did he—"

The bus lurched and screeched to a stop. "This is us," Krisda said.

They tumbled out into the gentle night. Mike jogged to catch up to his roommates. Austin and Shep fell in behind, and they started up the hill, surrounded by jungle sounds. It was dark most of the way, until they got close enough to see the lamp with its halo of mosquitos guarding the shortcut through the basketball court. Then they knew they were home.

Mike wasn't really worried about Austin beating him up. If anything, Austin was the one who had reason to worry, because—whatever Jason Keen had paid him—Mrs. Watkins would flip her lid if she found out.

Austin wasn't the only one with a secret, though. Back in their room, getting ready for bed, Mike burned with the need to tell someone. What was the fun of being a secret agent if you couldn't tell anyone?

But Jason Keen said his country needed him, and that should be enough. Then there was that other thing, the hope he mustn't allow himself even to think out loud. Mr. Keen hadn't come right out and said it. But he hadn't *not* said it, either.

So, Mike would carry his secret alone. He carried it down to breakfast and stirred it around in his cornflakes while Mrs. Watkins small-talked over his head. He carried it with him to school, through crowds of kids he didn't really know. The secret surrounded him like a bubble. It protected him from harm and happiness, not letting anything in or out. He even carried it to Malay class, where it left his body and hovered around the room looking for someone else to possess, someone more worthy, while Mike lost himself in the simple cadence of syllables trundling off his tongue. But the secret always came back to Mike in the end.

He carried it with him even on the miserable ride home. The sick feeling in his stomach got even sicker as the van circled the roundabout on Holland Road and approached the turn-off. That was when Mike saw the car.

Parked on a dirt lay-by under the shade of a big tree, just a few yards away from the Soda Pop Man. A red Mustang convertible. The top was up, but Mike didn't need to see inside to know who the driver was.

After the van pulled up in front of the hostel, Mike hung back while the others headed for the dorms at different speeds, some walking lackadaisically, some sprinting like maniacs. He knew Mrs. Watkins would be lurking near the entrance to greet them, like she always did. He pretended to follow the crowd, then at the last second veered off toward the basketball court, breaking into a run.

At the shortcut he stopped and crouched low, looking back through the leafy undergrowth. Nobody was following him. It took a few seconds more to hide his schoolbooks inside a bush and cover them with dead leaves, before trotting down the path into the deserted road.

Far off, the traffic sounded like a rushing stream, but here, in the jungly shade, he was greeted by the calls of birds. Dappled by sunlight through the canopy of leaves, he could have been on a great adventure, if he wasn't so nervous. He whistled the melody to "Kung Fu Fighting," and it gave him courage as he neared the traffic at the end of the long drive.

The Soda Pop Man was set up in his usual place in the shade, sitting on a wooden crate behind his pushcart. A few yards away, the red Mustang purred. Mike dug into his pocket for what was left of his lunch money, trying not to look at the car.

"Hi. How much is a Coke?"

The Soda Pop Man shook his head. "No Coke. Finish already. Orange and grape only."

"Grape, then."

"Special price for you, my friend. One dollar, okay?"

Mike fished a limp bill out of his pocket and handed it over. He knew he was paying the *ang moh* price but didn't feel like haggling. There was too much else on his mind.

The Soda Pop Man put on a show, flipping the lid of his cooler open and whisking out a bottle dripping with ice water, flicking off the bottle cap with one hand and whipping out a plastic bag with the other. Purple liquid gurgled and gushed. It all happened in seconds. The Soda Pop Man grinned as he handed Mike a plastic bag full of grape soda dangling on a string. The empty bottle clinked as it slid into a crate.

"*Terima kasih.* Thank you," said Mike.

The Soda Pop Man dipped his head like a circus performer taking a bow. Then he sat down behind his pushcart again and lost himself in his dreams.

For a minute or two Mike wandered back and forth along the lay-by, kicking at rocks and sucking grape soda through a straw. He ambled past the car, then meandered back. At a bus stop a few yards down the road, a couple of old ladies were peering at him through the blur of traffic.

"So, you showed up," a voice said. The window of the Mustang was rolled down, and a tattooed arm rested on the door. "Hop in. Let's go for a ride."

Mike hesitated. Riding in a car with strangers was high on the list of punishable offenses. But Mr. Keen wasn't *exactly* a stranger.

"Mike? Get in the car."

Mike held the plastic baggie against his teeth and squeezed, forcing the last of the grape soda into his mouth. He stuffed the wet bag into his pocket and scampered around to the other side. He had barely slid into the passenger seat when the Mustang peeled off into traffic.

Jason Keen drove with his foot flat on the gas, weaving in and out of traffic like a race car driver. "What language do you take in school?" he said, shifting gears. They whizzed past taxis and buses and motor scooters. Trees and buildings and pedestrians melted into a blur.

Mike hadn't expected to be questioned about school. For a second, he thought Mr. Keen must be making fun of him, and this whole thing was a joke. But the man's face was expressionless, staring straight ahead as he drove.

"I take Malay with Mr. Shani."

Mr. Keen nodded. "I thought so. I need you to switch to Mandarin."

"What? Why?"

Mr. Keen drummed his fingers against the steering wheel. "*Need-to-know*, Mike."

"But I'm good at Malay! It'll hurt Mr. Shani's feelings if I switch."

"Feelings," Mr. Keen said. He just left the word out there to die, like there was nothing else to say. "He'll get over it, Mike. Can you do this for your country, or not?"

"But—"

"The other day you seemed willing to make the sacrifice. But if I was wrong about you, then..."

20

"Okay," said Mike. "Okay, I'll switch. I just don't get the big deal about Mandarin. Nobody tells me anything."

Mr. Keen pressed a button on the dash, and the mechanical roof buzzed open. A blast of wind and sunlight came gushing in.

"You help me, I'll help you, Mike. That's how this works. But I need to know you're on board."

Jason Keen switched gears again, and the car exploded into hyperspace, tires peeling as they rounded a bend. Mike put both hands on the dash and held on, feeling a thrill as his heart leapt into his throat.

"Just follow instructions, and you'll be fine!" Jason Keen shouted over the roar of the wind. "Just be yourself!"

He took his foot off the gas, and they glided down the road as the engine purred. Mike was surprised to find they were back where they started, drifting to a stop next the Soda Pop Man.

Mike reached for the door handle, but Mr. Keen stopped him. "Look in the glove compartment," he said.

Mike did as he was told. Inside was a glossy brochure for the Lion City Martial Arts Academy.

"We need a better cover for our meetings," Mr. Keen explained. "This way I can pick you up at school."

"Tae Kwon Do?" The brochure trembled in Mike's hand. "But what about Mrs. Watkins. Won't she—"

"The arrangements have already been made. It's an official extracurricular activity." Mr. Keen lay a hand on Mike's shoulder. "Next time I want to hear all about Mandarin class. Got it?"

Mike folded the brochure and creased it to fit in his pocket. "But why me?"

"*Need-to-know*, Mike."

"You have to tell me why."

Jason Keen looked at him hard. "Because you need me as much as I need you. Because I *trust* you, okay? You're the only one who can do this. Are you in or out?"

There was no place to hide from the cerulean authority of his eyes. Mike stepped out of the car and shut the door. Darting across the road between blurs of speeding cars, he didn't look back.

Chapter 7

As the rest of the class stampeded out to recess, Mike stayed behind to break the news to Mr. Shani. Luckily, the teacher didn't take it personally.

"Mandarin also good," said Mr. Shani. "But why now, Mike?"

"My parents made me," said Mike. "Because we might be moving to China."

It was only half a lie. His parents were in the Foreign Service, so they *might* move to China one day.

Mr. Shani shook his head gently in commiseration. "You Americans, always moving, lah."

"Plus, there's billions more people to talk to," added Mike.

"Ah, this true. Good luck, Mike."

"*Terima kasih*, Mr. Shani."

"*Sama-sama*. But first must get form signed."

"Oh. There's a form?"

Mr. Shani didn't have a copy of the form on him, so Mike had to go to the office to get one. This was in a different part of the school that Mike didn't know well, because he never got in enough trouble to get sent to the office. It took half his morning break just to find the place.

The school secretary greeted him with a frown. "Very bad one ah? What you did?"

"Nothing!"

"Go sit." She pointed to the Time-Out bench, where a police line-up of surly sixth-graders was waiting for their turn to get hollered at.

"But I didn't do anything! Mr. Shani sent me to get a form."

"Why early don't say?" She shook her head at him and clicked her tongue. "What form you need?"

Mike told her, and the secretary disappeared behind a huge filing cabinet. A fly buzzed around the edge of a window as he waited. The sixth-grade delinquents were watching him closely, as if they knew he was involved in a secret conspiracy. He felt himself sinking deeper into the quicksand of his own lies. Trapped, just like the fly.

"Ah, this one can." The secretary licked her finger, peeled a mimeographed sheet of paper out of a manila folder and laid it on the counter. Her red-polished fingernail tapped a dotted line at the bottom of the page. "Parent must sign."

The Schedule Change Request form was official-looking and intimidating, with some of the words typed extra hard as if the typist was in a bad mood.

"But my parents don't live here," said Mike.

She gave him a sorrowful look. "Who take care of you? Guardian also can sign."

Mike hadn't expected that he would have to involve Mrs. Watkins. The thought of lying to her gave him a queasy feeling. "Thanks."

Mike exited through the glass doors into the blinding sunlight. The shock of the heat made him dizzy. He collapsed onto a bench next to a potted tree and buried his face in his hands. Things were getting out of control. He wished he could go back in time, but it was too late to undo the lies he had already told.

Recess was over, and the open-air walkways were deserted except for a scraggly line of third-graders snaking its way to the library. Which gave Mike the only good idea he'd had all day. He waited for the last kid in line to pass by, then fell in behind like an overgrown mascot. Nobody seemed to mind, least of all the little kids in front of him, who turned around and laughed. Mike shushed them with a finger to his lips.

Once inside the library, he peeled off to the card catalog and looked for the "S" drawer. S is for spy. His shaky fingers flipped through the index cards as his heart beat loud in his ears. He didn't notice the librarian sneaking up on him until it was too late.

"Well, look what the cat dragged in," she said.

Mike jumped, slamming the card-drawer shut on his thumb.

"Are you all right?"

"I'm fine," said Mike, resisting the urge to jam his thumb into his mouth.

Mrs. Range folded her burly arms and narrowed her eyes at him. "Are you where you're supposed to be?"

"Um. Not exactly."

"Bless your *heart*. Better let me help you, then."

Mike glanced left and right, lowered his voice to a near whisper. "Have you got any books on spies?"

"More than you can shake a stick at," said Mrs. Range, leading him into a forest of shelves in the 300s section. "Anything in particular about spies?"

"Like… how to be one."

She looked at him out of the corner of her eye. "Why. Thinking of signing up?"

Mike, pretending not to hear, dropped to his knees and started searching through the books on the bottom shelf.

"Right." Mrs. Range put her librarian glasses back on. "Got to get back to my rat-killing. Just holler if you need me."

Mike waited for the striped cotton dress to disappear around the stacks before he allowed himself to breathe again. How much had he given away? Did the librarian suspect something? Mrs. Range attended the same church as Mike on Sundays, but he didn't know if this was a good thing or a bad thing. What if she started blabbing to the other church ladies? Worse yet, what if she ratted him out to Pastor Bob?

Mike found what he was looking for—*The Boy's Book of Spy Craft*—which he chose partly for its shape and size. It was just big enough to conceal the Schedule Change Request form between its pages.

That night during Study Hour, after he finished his math problems, Mike took out his colored pencils and tried working on his comic book. He had finally got the characters right—the boy secret agent was nerdy and a little bit cool, and the President looked like a passable Richard Nixon. But now the story itself was starting to seem silly and unbelievable. He shoved the whole mess into his desk drawer without

24

even putting the colored pencils back in their box. He didn't have time anymore for childish make-believe.

He checked over his shoulder before reaching for *The Boy's Book of Spy Craft*. Krisda was reading, and Bryan was struggling miserably with a Language Arts essay. It was safe for Mike to pull out the Schedule Change Request form and study what he had completed so far. He worried that his printing was too neat and careful to look like an adult's handwriting, but it would have to do. The only thing left was the hardest part.

Luckily, he still had the letter Mrs. Watkins had sent him, welcoming him to the Christian Children's Hostel. He used the signature as a model, first tracing it, then practicing it freehand over and over, mouthing the name silently as he wrote. *Betty Watkins. Betty Watkins. Betty Watkins.*

It was better not to think too much about what he was doing. It was possibly a crime, and certainly against the school rules. But what choice did he have? If he asked Mrs. Watkins for permission, she would want to know the reasons. She would insist on an explanation that made sense. And even then, no matter what he came up with, there was no guarantee that she would believe him. She might still refuse to sign the form, and then the whole mission, whatever it was, would be in jeopardy. There might be lives at stake. Maybe even…

At eight o'clock precisely, stereos up and down the hall blasted simultaneously, signaling the end of Study Hour. Krisda leaped off his bed like Superman in a sarong, his outstretched fingers missing the blades of the ceiling fan by an inch.

Bryan turned up the volume. He danced and dodged across the room, grinning, while Krisda feinted left and right, boxing the air, singing the words to "Muhammad Ali."

Mike scribbled the signature one last time on the dotted line, then quickly hid the evidence between the pages of his book.

Chapter 8

After Mr. Ibrahim dropped them off at school, Mike didn't go straight to his Learning Community like he was supposed to. Those days of better angels, of being good, were over. Now he weaved his way through enemy territory, his white school shirt damp with sweat, *The Boy's Book of Spy Craft* gripped tightly at his side.

His hand shook horribly when he passed the Schedule Change Request form across the counter. The school secretary's eyes scanned the paper up and down, left to right, like a pair of mechanical camera lenses. A drop of sweat formed on Mike's temple and started sliding down his cheek; it tickled, but he didn't brush it away, for fear the gesture might betray him.

"Very good, very good," said the secretary.

Mike felt a cleansing wave of relief and gratitude rushing through his body. He was light-headed with joy. "*Xie xie. Terima kasih.* Thank you," he said, covering all three official languages at once.

"Now only need counselor signature."

"What?!" Mike gasped. "But—but—you didn't say anything—"

"Form say. On back. See?" She flipped the page over and tapped a dotted line with her painted fingernail.

Mike stared. How could he have been so stupid? All his hard work crashing to ruin because of one tiny, overlooked detail.

"No problem," said the secretary. "Miss Kumar coming now."

Of all the school staff, Miss Kumar was the most feared. She could see into a boy's soul. She would tell you exactly what you were feeling and explain the reasons why. After two minutes, she knew more about you than you knew yourself. "Never mind," said Mike, willing himself not to cry. "It was a dumb idea. I'll just stick with Malay."

"What talking you?" The secretary looked like she might slap him. "Want switch to Mandarin or not?"

Miss Kumar didn't walk so much as glide in her flowing sari, as if she was riding on clouds. In this way she miraculously passed through the glass doors, carrying a hot cup of tea in both hands.

"Mike, I'm so glad to see you!" said Miss Kumar, smiling at him like he was the only boy in the universe. Her accent sounded almost English, except for a musical lilt that turned her syllables into the notes of a song.

"Make trouble, this one," said the secretary, wagging her finger at Mike. "Need form signed, but now don't want."

"Oh?" Miss Kumar's smile faltered. "Let's have a chat then, shall we?" She glided down the hall, and Mike followed like an unwilling acolyte, until they came to her office door. Miss Kumar looked down on him from the heights of her cloud, cradling the cup of tea in her hands. "Pardon my tea, Mike," she said. "Would you mind?"

"Huh?"

"Open the door, please."

Mike blushed as his fingers fumbled with the door knob.

Miss Kumar's office was small but bright with sunlight. A window behind her desk looked out on a patch of trees, and the walls were lined with books on psychology. Miss Kumar ushered Mike into a cushioned chair, then took a seat behind her desk, resting the cup of tea in front of her. "I'm actually really glad you stopped by, Mike. I've been meaning to have a chat—so tell me, how are you holding up?"

Name, rank, and serial number. That was all he was obliged to give, according to the articles of the Geneva Convention. "Fine," he said.

But Miss Kumar had ways of making you talk. "Really?" Her voice was infused with kindness, the red dot on her forehead crinkling in sympathy. "I imagine it must be a tough time for you, with everything that's going on."

Mike swallowed at the lump growing in his throat. But he kept his lips tightly closed. It occurred to him that the Geneva Convention didn't apply to secret agents. Spies could be tortured, even taken out and shot.

Miss Kumar took a sip of her tea, and the cup made a clinking sound as she replaced it in the saucer. "Well then, tell me about this form that needs signing."

Mike felt a pressure behind his eyes, like a dam about to burst. He gripped *The Boy's Book of Spy Craft* tightly on his lap. Whatever happened, he couldn't let her see the childish signature on the form. "No, it's okay," he said.

Miss Kumar looked puzzled. "You wanted to switch to Mandarin, didn't you?"

Mike stared. His tongue felt like a dry slab, too numb to speak.

"Mr. Shani mentioned it me," said Miss Kumar, tilting her head in apology. "Perhaps you should give the form to me, Mike. Since Mrs. Watkins took the trouble to sign it."

Mike felt his resolve breaking down. Maybe if he surrendered peacefully, they would go easy on him. After a full confession, he would be punished, and then forgiven. He opened *The Boy's Book of Spy Craft* on his lap and extracted the Schedule Change Request form. The paper rustled for a few seconds in his shaky fingers, then drifted like a windblown feather onto the desk.

He waited for judgement to fall. But strangely, nothing happened. Miss Kumar wasn't finished with him yet.

"I do have some concerns about you switching languages so late in the term," she said, without even looking at the form. "Especially a boy in your situation."

A boy in your situation. A hopeless case.

"I'm inclined to give Mrs. Watkins a ring to discuss this with her."

"No!" said Mike. "I mean, you don't need to. I've changed my mind. I'll stick with Malay."

They both looked at the telephone sitting on the corner of the desk. It was the old-fashioned clunky kind with a rotary dial—a brute weapon. "But Mrs. Watkins is making the request on your behalf," said Miss Kumar. "If anyone's mind is going to change, it must be hers. Do you see my predicament, Mike? As your guardian, it's *her* decision."

Mike nodded mutely. Now that his doom was sealed, he felt strangely calm.

Miss Kumar gave him a small sympathetic smile. "Not to worry, Mike. Why don't you leave this with me?"

Mike watched the form disappear unceremoniously into her desk drawer. He felt a piece of himself going into the dark along with it, to sequester there forever among Miss Kumar's paper clips.

"Enough about that for now," said Miss Kumar, picking up her tea. "Tell me, how are you getting on?"

"Fine."

"You're making friends?"

Mike shrugged. "Bryan's okay. And Krisda."

Miss Kumar's red dot crinkled slightly. "Your roommates, is it? Yes, I can see the hostel must be a special place. Friends ready-made, like brothers almost."

Mike mentally kicked himself. Of *course* Bryan and Krisda didn't count. Having roommates wasn't the same as having friends. It didn't save you from being a hopeless case.

Mike knew he was beaten. A few minutes ago, he had been a man with a mission. Now, he slumped in his chair. There was nothing left but to let justice run its course.

"I've so enjoyed our little chat, Mike," said Miss Kumar, opening up her appointment book. "You must come back again soon. Shall we say, next week?"

Chapter 9

On his way to class, Mike stopped off at the boys' room to throw up. The detour caused him to be late for homeroom. Mr. Stone was halfway through the morning announcements and didn't even look at Mike when he came in.

"Don't forget, auditions for the musical are coming up. It's *Jesus Christ Superstar* this year, so don't miss your chance at stardom!"

Some kids groaned, others laughed. Mike collapsed into a seat at the back of the room—which technically wasn't a room but one of several "pods" that made up the Learning Community—and wiped some vomit off his chin.

Roger Tan raised his hand. "If we try out, does that mean we have to sing?"

Mr. Stone was deadpan. "Well, Roger, seeing how it *is* a musical, there might be some singing, yes."

A bunch of kids laughed. Mr. Stone was an Australian and the coolest teacher in school. Everybody liked him.

"Sign-up sheets are posted on the bulletin board. Don't forget!"

Mike made a cradle of his arms and put his head down on the desk. He was almost dozing off when the classes started to change. There were no bells at this school, everybody just randomly guessed when the end of the period came. Mike saw the other kids leaving, and he stood up groggily.

"Hang on a minute, Mike-o. Got a question for ya."

Mike edged toward the teacher's desk. "Yes, sir?"

Mr. Stone frowned. "You right, mate? You look a bit green around the gills."

"I'm okay." Mike stuffed his hands in his pockets.

"Listen, I didn't want to put you on the spot just now, but I really think you should sign up for an audition."

"*Me?* Why?"

"Because you've got a great voice, that's why. And you might even have some fun. You do *like* singing, don't you?"

Mike shrugged sheepishly. "Sort of," he admitted.

"Well, think about it, alright?"

"Okay."

Mr. Stone slapped Mike's shoulder playfully. "Good on yer, Mike-o." He turned to erase the blackboard, then suddenly changed his mind. "Oh, Mike? One other thing…"

One other thing. Just like in the movies, when the detective waits for the bad guy to let his guard down, then springs the trap.

"About this switch to Mandarin…I've spoken to Mr. Shani and Mrs. Lee. It's a bit of a dog's breakfast, but we reckon you're good to go."

Mike swallowed the bile in the back of his throat, pushing his hands deeper into his pockets. "But—"

"Haven't changed your mind, have you?"

"But what about the form? Miss Kumar said—"

"Strewth, Mike-o, you need to relax! We'll do the form later. Just go to class and enjoy yourself. Mrs. Lee's expecting you."

Something weird was going on, this conspiracy of teachers plotting behind his back, but he didn't have time to think about it now. The pod was filling up with kids again, and Mike was already late to his first period class. "Thanks, Mr. Stone."

"No worries, mate. And don't forget to sign up!"

The Learning Community was a hive of activity, boys and girls crossing in every direction from one pod to another, yammering and horsing around. Mike passed the bulletin board and saw the shiny cardboard lettering: *Be a Super-Star!* The sign-up sheet was still empty.

Gamma Learning Community was almost exactly the same as Beta Learning Community, except they had a Mandarin pod instead of a Malay pod. When Mike arrived, most kids were already settled in their pods around the perimeter of the giant hexagon. Mike was the solitary figure in the middle, walking across empty space.

"Boy and girl, we have new student," the old lady announced. Mrs. Lee made him come to the front of the class and stand there like an idiot. There were only six other kids, mostly girls. The only other boy sat at a table near the back, looking bored.

"Welcome, Mike. Today we practice Chinese calligraphy. You can sit next to Jin Kim."

Mike trudged to the table in the back and slid into a chair next to the boy. Jin Kim barely looked at him. "Hi," said Mike.

There were brushes laid out on the table, and rolls of paper, and a dollop of black ink in a tiny porcelain bowl. Everybody was quietly working, and Mrs. Lee was walking around the tables. Mike watched what the boy was doing, and tried to do the same—dipping his brush in the ink, then making careful strokes on the paper.

Jin Kim made a face and clicked his tongue. "*Ang moh*, what you doing?"

"Huh?"

"Can you dun copy me."

"What?"

"Why you so blur, man? Don't copy me!"

"I'm not!" said Mike, which technically wasn't true. "How am I supposed to learn, then?"

Jin Kim shrugged. "Neh mind, this school got no rules, everything *bo cheng hu*, make me crazy one! Copy if you want, lor."

Stealing glances at the boy between brush strokes, Mike felt a tightening in his throat. Maybe it was an aftereffect of throwing up this morning, or maybe he was coming down with the flu. Jin Kim's silky black hair fell across his eyes, and he kept brushing it back with his free hand. His tongue lodged in the corner of his mouth as he tried to get the brushstrokes right. He caught Mike looking, and scowled. "Never see before?"

Mike's face burned. "Sorry. I was just—"

"Why you here anyhow?" said Jin Kim. "This not your class."

"Yes, it is. I switched from Malay."

"What for, man? Malay so easy one!"

Mike shrugged.

"Parents make you, ah?"

"No. My parents aren't around."

The boy's eyebrows went up, his mouth hung agape. "Who take care of you? Got aunties or what?"

"I'm staying at a hostel."

"Eh? That like a orphanage, is it?"

Mike glared at him. "It's nothing like that!" His hand was shaking, sprinkling droplets of ink on the table. "I'm not an orphan."

"Relak, man! I only asking, lah."

Jin Kim went back to his work, glancing at Mike sideways. Mike tried to mop up the spilled ink with his thumb, but only managed to smear it.

"Why then?" said Jin Kim.

"Why what?" said Mike, wiping his inky hand on his pants.

"What for your parents leave you?"

Mike tried to steady his breathing, which was coming out in ragged gasps. "They didn't *leave* me."

"Then what?" Jin Kim clicked his tongue. "You did something bad?"

What happened next surprised even Mike. He was not normally a violent person. But somehow the brush came to life in his hand, whipping an arc of ink across the table.

"*Wah piang* eh!" Jin Kim jumped up, rubbing at the splotches on his white school shirt. "Look what you did!"

Kids were turning in their seats to look. "Why you boys shouting lai dat?" said Mrs. Lee, helicoptering over to their table.

Mike lowered his burning face closer to his paper, adding brush-strokes to his pictogram to make a spaceship.

Jin Kim pointed his finger at Mike. "*Pai kia* this one! Look my shirt. He sabo me!"

Mrs. Lee folded her arms and scowled. "Very good, very good, who ask you? All the time play and don't listen."

"Wah, my fault is it? How can?!"

"Want I talk to your mother ah?"

33

Jin Kim fumed but didn't say any more until Mrs. Lee had helicop-
tered away back to the front of the room.

"*Ang moh*, you make trouble for me."

Mike added an enemy spaceship to his picture and blew it to
smithereens. His breath was still coming out shaky, but the brush had
stopped its trembling, licking the paper now with quick deft strokes.

"Think you very talent one, ha?" Jin Kim curled his fingers into a
fist. "You wait, man. I humtum you good!"

Chapter 10

Mike's nerves were on edge. A ring of sweat darkened his collar, and his pants were stained with ink. He combed his sweaty hair with his fingers as he hobbled along the sidewalk, searching the carpool lane for the Volkswagen bus. What he found instead was Jason Keen, leaning against the door of a red Ford Mustang.

Mike ducked behind a pillar. He didn't ask himself what he was so afraid of. He just knew he didn't want to be a secret agent. Not today. He peered around the pillar long enough to read the logo newly painted on the Mustang's side—*Lion City Martial Arts Academy*. For a second Mr. Keen seemed to look straight through him, without seeing him at all. As if God had made him invisible.

Mike whispered a prayer as he swam through the crowd upstream. He spotted the old Volkswagen bus parked a few cars down and felt a surge of relief. He ached to sit down, to let his head rest against the window, to dream himself home. But as he climbed into the van, Mr. Ibrahim said: "Mike, teacher looking for you."

Mike missed his footing, grabbed a seat-back to steady himself. "What teacher?"

Mr. Ibrahim gestured with a nod of his head. "That one. Martial Arts teacher."

Mike crawled over a third-grader's legs and ducked behind the seat. "It's okay, Mr. Ibrahim, no Tae Kwon Do today."

The driver squinted at him dubiously. Mike smiled back like nothing was wrong, sliding down further in his seat until his knees sank into the backrest in front. He stayed that way, folded up like a contortionist, as the van filled with children. Danny, the third-grader, was watching him the whole time. "You're really skipping class?" he whispered.

"Sort of," said Mike, keeping his voice low. But he felt a responsibility to set a good example, so he added: "I'll probably get in trouble for it."

Danny's mouth hung open, and he looked at Mike with shining eyes. Having a third-grader look up to you was like being kidnapped by aliens from outer space and put in an alien zoo: the aliens didn't know you were a dork. They didn't know you were a hopeless case. They thought you were just a normal specimen, and the sign on your cage said simply: *Human Being.*

"Danny, you see the red car?"

Danny nodded.

"The man in the Hawaiian shirt. Is he still there?"

"He's coming this way," said Danny. Then he frowned at Mike and said seriously: "You're in a *lot* of trouble, aren't you?"

Mike shifted into the space between the seats, squeezing himself small until he squatted on the floor. "Don't tell him I'm here."

"I won't," Danny whispered back.

Mike hugged his knees and squeezed his eyes shut. Sweat tickled his face, and his scalp itched, but he didn't dare move a muscle. Not until the van door slid shut, and the engine sputtered to life, and Bryan and Krisda broke into a chorus of "Kung Fu Fighting." Mr. Ibrahim stepped on the gas, and the van peeled away from the curb faster than usual.

Mike let out a long breath as the movement of air cooled the sweat on his face. Limp with exhaustion, he struggled to get himself unstuck from between the seats. Danny pulled on his arm to help him. For a second, Mike thought he was free.

But the eyes in the rearview mirror were watching him. Mike answered Mr. Ibrahim's gaze with a silent plea: *Don't tell Mrs. Watkins.*

He leaned his head against the window glass and closed his burning eyes. All he wanted to do was sleep. But Danny wasn't going to let him off the hook that easy. The third-grader had just saved Mike's butt, and he wanted something in return. "Can you play with me when we get home?" said Danny.

* * *

36

Pock.....Tick. Pock..... Tick. Pock..... Tick. Pock...... Tick. WHAM!

A blur of white light shot off Mike's paddle and shaved the far left corner of the table. Danny dived for it and missed. The ball went on an erratic tour of the patio, ricocheting off walls and chair-backs, bouncing down the steps onto the concrete pavement of the basketball court.

"Dang!" The ball got kicked by somebody's shoe, and Danny scurried after it. Then Austin kicked it away on purpose, and Danny lost his temper. "Cut it out, you guys!"

Shirts and Skins paused their game. Shep scooped up the ping-pong ball and dropped it in Danny's hand. "Sorry, Danny. Better keep it out of our game though, or it might get stepped on."

The basketball game started up again, and Danny ran back to the ping-pong table with storm clouds on his face. "Jerks!"

"Match point," said Mike.

Danny tossed the ball. It bounced on Mike's side of the table and landed lightly in his hand.

Mike was feeling better after his shower. The last traces of school were cleansed from his body, and the fresh shorts and T-shirt hung lightly on him, and his feet could finally breathe again after being imprisoned in cheap sneakers all day. It made him feel like a brand-new person, making a clean start. He tossed the ball up and down in his palm a couple of times, enjoying the suspense as Danny crouched in a ninja stance on the other side of the table. The sounds of skidding feet, the shouts from the basketball court, didn't distract him. His concentration was perfect. He knew just how much spin he wanted to put on his serve, and he was already relishing Danny's surprise. Then he heard a voice call his name.

"Mike, could you come with me, please?"

It was the voice of Trouble. Mrs. Watkins stood framed in the French doors that were always kept open. Danny was gaping. The action on the basketball court went quiet as Shirts and Skins turned to look.

A lump lodged in Mike's throat. He lay the ping-pong paddle carefully on top of the ball and followed Mrs. Watkins through the French doors, his downcast eyes watching the blurry heels of her flip-flop sandals. They passed through the deserted dining room, then the TV room, and out the other side. The two main buildings were connected by a roof that sheltered the space between, and it was there, beside the outdoor table, that Mrs. Watkins stopped and turned.

"Mike, is there anything you want to tell me?"

The lump in Mike's throat tightened as he thought of the forgery. Miss Kumar must have called her. But he felt giddy with the relief of confession as the words spilled out of him. "It was because of the cheeseburgers. Things just happened all of a sudden. I couldn't get out of it."

Mrs. Watkins' laser-beam eyes seemed to readjust themselves behind the cage of her glasses. For a second, she looked perplexed. Then the eyes regained their focus, the laser beams burning and sizzling into his brain. "Things just *happened?* This is your explanation for skipping Tae Kwon Do class?"

"What?" *Shut up shut up shut up.* "Oh, that," said Mike.

Mrs. Watkins folded her arms. Which was never a good sign. "Mike, we *talked* about this," she said. "Tae Kwon Do is an extra-curricular activity. It deserves your best effort. Mr. Keen waited for you at school for almost an hour."

Mike winced. "I guess I forgot."

"Well, I think you should apologize, don't you?"

"Yes ma'am," said Mike. "I'm really sorry."

"Not to me," said Mrs. Watkins. "To your Martial Arts teacher."

"Huh?"

That was when Mike noticed the red Mustang in the driveway. It was half-hidden by a tree, but the logo painted on its door was unmistakable. *Lion City Martial Arts Academy.* His heart sickened as he followed Mrs. Watkins inside.

The man in the Hawaiian shirt was sitting on a rattan sofa in the assembly room. Seeing him there made Mike want to squirm, though he tried not to show it. There was something awful about Jason Keen even being here in the room where they prayed together, where Mrs. Watkins read from her Bible, where they sang in harmony to the strum of Shep's guitar.

38

But Mr. Keen stood up awkwardly when they entered, rubbing his hands like he didn't know what to do with them, and Mike felt bad for his unkind thoughts. "Sorry, Mr. Keen," he said. "I forgot."

Mr. Keen stretched his face into a smile. "No harm done."

"Go put your shoes on, Mike," said Mrs. Watkins, before turning to Jason Keen again and offering her hand to shake. "You have my apologies, too, Mr. Keen. Mike is usually such a *responsible* boy."

If there had been a hole in the floor, Mike would have crawled inside it. But then the shame gave way to another feeling as he padded up the stairs, trying to name what this other feeling was, like cold fingers wrapping around his heart.

Chapter 11

The Mustang turned into an alley and purred to a stop between two dilapidated warehouses. Mike guessed from the smell that they were somewhere near the river. Chinatown. A rat leapt off the top of an oil drum and scampered under a pile of debris. Further down the alley, a team of shirtless men was loading crates of fish onto the back of a truck. "I thought you were supposed to teach me Tae Kwon Do," said Mike.

Mr. Keen shot him a look before stepping out of the car. He peeled a magnetic strip off the Mustang's door and tossed it behind the driver's seat. Mike stared at the *Martial Arts Academy* logo in disgust. "You mean it's only fake?"

Mr. Keen crossed in front of the car toward the warehouse on the left, walking fast. Mike had to jump out of the car and run to catch up. *Ho Chin Importing Ltd.*, in English and Chinese, was painted above a rusted door, which squealed on its hinges when Mr. Keen pulled it open. A steep flight of stairs ascended in front of them, dark except for a single bulb hanging above the top landing. Mr. Keen took the stairs two at a time as Mike jogged behind.

The silence was starting to scare him a little. Mr. Keen hadn't spoken a word since they'd left the hostel.

"Sorry about today," said Mike, breathing hard, as he neared the top landing.

Mr. Keen looked down at him, unsmiling. The dangling lightbulb cast sharp shadows down the length of the man's face. He stood between a pair of almost identical doors. From the door on the left came the muffled groans and shouts of some terrible human ordeal. The slap of bare feet on a concrete floor. A fist hitting flesh. A grunt of pain.

But it was the door on the right that Mr. Keen opened. The room was harshly lit, with worn-out benches lining its perimeter, and clothes hanging from hooks on the peeling walls. Mr. Keen led the way through the changing room into a cramped office in the back. He turned and stood next to an old battered desk, looking hard at Mike. The boy hovered just inside the door, biting his thumbnail. "I'm sorry," Mike said. "I won't forget again."

Still Mr. Keen didn't say anything. The cold blue eyes pierced Mike to the heart, and he squirmed like a bug on a pin.

Mr. Keen unbuckled his belt. "Do you have any idea how dangerous it is for me to show up at the hostel uninvited?" The belt slithered through the loops of his chino pants. Thick brown leather, an inch and a half wide. "Do you understand how close you came to jeopardizing *everything?*"

Mike's mouth went suddenly dry. A stammered apology got caught in his throat, and he tried to swallow it down.

Mr. Keen dropped the belt onto the desktop, where it lay like a half-killed snake, inert but dangerous. He started to unbutton his shirt. "You can change in there," he said, nodding toward the changing room. "Hook 13."

Mike found his spot on the wall—the only empty hook. His breath was coming out shaky, and he leaned his forehead against the crumbling plaster and closed his eyes. He had a sudden impulse to run away. A short dash to the stairwell, a sprint down the alley. But then what? He didn't even know which bus to take home, and anyway, Mrs. Watkins would just send him right back.

Mike slipped out of his shorts and T-shirt and hung them from the hook. On the bench below, a white uniform lay neatly folded. The loose-fitting pants and tunic felt rough against his skin when he put them on. He wrapped the cloth belt around his waist and attempted to tie it with a knot.

"Not like that," said Mr. Keen, behind him. "Let me help you." He wore the same uniform as Mike, but with the belt dyed black. He took the belt off now to show Mike the correct way to tie it. Mike's hands fumbled a lot, and he had to start over a few times before he got it right.

"I flunked PE once," said Mike, looking at the floor. "Just so you know."

"You'll be fine."

"*Nobody* flunks PE. Except me."

"Look at me, Mike. I'm going to show you how to bow."

"Huh?" Mike looked up. "What for?"

"*Charyut!*" Mr. Keen's body stood suddenly straight, like a soldier called to attention.

Mike cringed. "What was *that?*"

"Attention position. Feet together, hands at your sides. Shoulders straight."

It felt weird, like he was a little boy playing soldier, but he did as he was instructed.

"Don't look at the floor, Mike, look at me. Head straight. That's better."

Mike held his position, and the weird feeling passed. His body was firm, lean and strong, poised like a spring.

"We bow at the waist," said Mr. Keen, bending down. "Hands to the side."

Mike followed his example, bending at the waist, watching closely everything Mr. Keen did.

"Don't *watch* me while your bowing, as if you don't trust me! Show some respect. Avert your eyes."

Mike tried again, bowing lower this time, keeping his head down.

"It begins with a bow and ends with a bow. You can mess up everything in between, but get the bow right. You understand?"

"Yes, sir," said Mike. "But—"

"You're ready now. Let's go."

"What do you mean? Ready for what? Where—"

Mr. Keen had already crossed the room and was opening the door to the stairs. Mike followed him out onto the landing with a sickening heart. "We're not going in *there*, are we?"

"I want you to meet my friend, Mr. Wong. He's expecting you."

Sighs of exhaustion and agony leaked out through the rusty door. Bodies colliding with bodies, limbs whacking limbs.

Mike gasped. "You're kidding, right?"

The door opened with a groan. Mr. Keen's hand pressed against the nape of Mike's neck, pushing him from behind.

"It begins with a bow and ends with a bow. Remember that, and you'll be fine."

"Wait. Don't leave me here!"

The door slammed behind him. Mike spun around and grabbed the handle, but the door stayed shut. His body slumped in defeat. He turned back around to face the room.

A regiment of boys stood watching him, all in white uniforms with different colored belts, lined up in disciplined rows. Mike realized, with a growing sense of unease, that he was the only *ang moh* there.

From behind the rows of boys, a tough-looking old man emerged. He stopped in front of Mike and studied him with a stern expression, until his steely eyes seemed to smile. *"Charyut!"* he barked.

The class stood to attention, and Mike did the same. Feet together, hands to the sides, shoulders straight. And slowly, as one, they bowed.

Chapter 12

This time it was Mike's turn to give the silent treatment, all the way to the Shangri-La Hotel. Mr. Keen had promised him a special treat—as if he thought Mike could be bought off with a cheeseburger.

"I thought you *liked* cheeseburgers," Mr. Keen said, pulling the Mustang into the hotel driveway. A doorman dressed like a Hollywood maharaja opened the passenger door, but Mike didn't get out.

"You're supposed to take me home," said Mike.

"Suit yourself," said Mr. Keen. "You can stay in the car."

A young valet approached the driver's side, and Mr. Keen pressed a wad of dollar bills into his hand. He cracked a joke in Malay as he got out of the car, and the valet laughed. Mike fumed, knowing the joke was about him.

"You tricked me," he said, following Mr. Keen into the lobby. Cold air stung his bare arms and legs as he spun through the revolving glass door. "Those kids almost *killed* me."

They crossed the polished marble floor to the elevator, and Mr. Keen pressed the button. "How did I trick you?"

"You didn't tell me I would have to fight black-belts. *Two* of them at once!"

The door dinged open. Mr. Keen suppressed a smile.

"You knew it, didn't you," Mike accused, following him into the elevator. "You *knew* the teacher would bust me for every little thing. I had to do pushups like a hundred times. On my *knuckles!*" He showed Mr. Keen his hands. His knuckles were bright red. "It still hurts where they kicked me," he said, touching a tender spot on his side. "I think my ribs got broke."

The elevator door dinged open again, and they stepped out into the open air of the poolside café. A waiter greeted them with menus, and they weaved their way between tables of Chinese businessmen and *ang moh* tourists. "Well, I heard a slightly different story," said Mr. Keen, taking a seat at a table near the poolside. He took his sunglasses off and studied the menu.

"What do you mean, different story?" Mike flumped into a rattan chair across from him. "What did you hear?"

Mr. Keen didn't look up from the menu. "I heard," he said, "you gave as good as you got."

Mike snorted in surprise. It obviously wasn't true. He had stumbled around like an idiot while the other boys clobbered him from every side.

"You got the bow right," Mr. Keen explained. "You comported yourself with dignity and respect. Mr. Wong wants you back."

"Really?"

"Starting tomorrow."

Mike opened his mouth to protest, but the waiter had come to take their order.

Mr. Keen barely touched his food. Mostly he just sipped his cocktail and watched Mike eat. He was already on his second drink, and Mike was barely halfway through his cheeseburger.

"Tell me about Mandarin class," said Mr. Keen.

Mike was about to take another bite of his cheeseburger, but paused. "I made the switch like you said, but…" A blob of ketchup seeped from his bun and splattered on the table. "I think I might be in trouble."

"What?" Mr. Keen's voice was as sharp as his look. "Why?"

Mike put the half-eaten cheeseburger down and wiped his fingers on his shorts. "Because of the stupid form," he said. "I think Miss Whatshername, the counselor, she knows about the signature. I tried my best, but it still looks like a kid did it."

Mr. Keen's voice was steady, his face expressionless. "You forged the signature?" He took his sunglasses off and pinched the bridge of his nose.

"I *had* to," Mike blurted. "What else was I supposed to do?"

"Jesus, Mike." Chair legs stuttered against the floor as Mr. Keen stood up. "Jesus Christ." He gestured to the bartender to catch his attention, and pointed to his empty glass. For a long minute he stood at the pool's edge, his back to Mike, staring into the dyed-blue water.

Mike pulled his feet up onto the seat and hugged his knees. "You shouldn't drink so much," he said. "The Bible says our bodies are the Lord's temple."

Mike clutched his knees tighter as Mr. Keen approached the table again. The tattooed tiger lurched across the man's thick bicep. His finger sliced the air and stopped an inch from Mike's face. "Don't press your luck, kid. Hear me?"

Mike cringed. He felt a need to say something smart-assed back, which happened with his dad sometimes when he was in trouble and could least afford it. But he kept his mouth tightly closed.

"Do you think we're *playing* here, Mike?" Mr. Keen sat down again and tipped the dregs of the cocktail glass into his mouth. The ice chinked against his teeth. "Do you think this is some kind of game?"

Mike kept his head down, gnawing nervously on his knee. He left teeth marks in the skin when he looked up. "Sorry. I just don't get what the big deal is. Why Mandarin?"

Mr. Keen seemed to calm down a little. "Forget it." He put his sunglasses back on. "Tell me about class. Did you make any friends?"

"It's stupid," said Mike. "We don't even learn anything, we just sit around painting with ink brushes."

"That's not what I asked you," said Mr. Keen. "I asked if you made any friends."

Mike impaled a French fry with his fork and dragged it under a mound of coleslaw to bury it. "Not really. There's only one other guy, and he's a jerk."

Mr. Keen drained his cocktail glass and set it back down. "I need you to take this opportunity to make friends, Mike."

"I *told* you, they're all girls except for—" Mike broke off and stared. "No way," he said.

"The boy's name is Jin Kim."

46

"Are you *kidding* me? The kid hates me!"

Mr. Keen was looking at him, but his sunglasses were on, and it was impossible to tell what the eyes were saying. "It won't kill you to make an effort, Mike."

"But *why*, if we hate each other?"

"*Need-to-know*, Mike. That's the mission."

"Nobody tells me anything!"

Mr. Keen ignored him. The waiter brought another cocktail and put the empty one on his tray. Mr. Keen said something to him in Malay.

"Domino only?" said the waiter. "Chess and checker also got."

"Just the dominos. And an ice cream for the boy."

Mike made a face. "We're going to play dominos?"

The waiter came back a minute later with an ice cream for Mike and a box of dominos. Mr. Keen waited for him to go away again before he lifted the lid off the box. "The communists are just biding their time, Mike." He turned the box upside down and dumped the dominos on the table. "You see this?" He held up a double-six to show Mike. "This is Vietnam."

"No, it's not. It's a domino."

Mr. Keen gave him a look. "Don't be a wise-ass." He stood the tile carefully on its edge.

"You're making a domino run," said Mike. He picked out a deuce-five and stood it up next to the double-six.

"Go ahead, if you're so smart," said Mr. Keen.

Mike laughed as he added more tiles to the run.

"That's enough," said Mr. Keen.

"No, wait!" Mike added more dominos to form a twisting tail that continued along the edge of the table before turning back toward the center. Dominos circled Mr. Keen's orangey cocktail and marched between the salt and pepper shakers.

"This isn't a game, Mike."

The smile fled from Mike's face, as if he'd been slapped.

Mr. Keen pointed a finger at the first domino in the line. "Do you remember what this one is?"

Mike slumped in his chair and gave a sullen glare.

"Vietnam," Mr. Keen answered for him. He pointed to the next domino in the line. "Laos." He pointed to each tile in turn, saying its name. "Cambodia. Thailand. Malaysia. Singapore. Indonesia… Are you beginning to get the picture?"

Mike stared at the ice cream melting in his dish.

"South Vietnam is next, Mike. It's only a matter of time."

"No, it's not," said Mike, looking up. "My parents are there."

"The communists in each of these countries are ready. They're organized."

"I was there last Christmas!"

"They're just waiting for the right time. When Saigon falls—"

Mike clutched the arms of his rattan chair like a fighter pilot preparing for a crash landing. He was shaking at the controls, and there was nothing he could do stop the impending explosion.

"Go ahead, Mike. Do it. Let's see what happens."

"No!" Mike leapt out of his chair, the table shuddered, and the whole domino world came tumbling down in cataclysmic ruin. "I don't care about your stinking dominos!"

The *ang moh* couple at the neighboring table turned to look. Mike ran across the rooftop terrace until there was nowhere left to run. He threw his arms over the concrete balustrade and held on. Somewhere far away a *muezzin* sang his call to prayer. Across the city, lights were being born in the last rays of the sun.

48

Chapter 13

For over a week now they had shared a table in Mandarin class. An invisible line down the middle separated Mike's side from Jin Kim's side, like a border between warring countries. They coexisted, not exactly in truce, but at least in a kind of ceasefire. Nothing crossed the invisible line. Until one day Jin Kim said, "*Ang moh*. Why you not sign up?"

The tip of Mike's pencil snapped. "What?"

Across the room, Mrs. Lee gave them a look.

Jin Kim lowered his head, pretended to concentrate on his paper. Mike did surgery on his broken pencil, twisting shreds of wood off the lead with his fingers.

"Why you not sign up?" Jin Kim whispered. "Today last day."

"What are you *talking* about?"

Jin Kim clicked his tongue. "You so blur like sotong! *Jesus Cry Superstar*, man. Next week auditions!"

Mike narrowed his eyes. "What's it to you?"

"Don't want to be the only boy, lah. Make me so lost form, everybody laughing at me."

Mike shrugged. "Maybe I don't want them laughing at me, either," he said. "Like I'm some kind of sissy."

"What talking you? Hollywood got plenty tough guy."

"Yeah, well, those guys aren't in middle school."

"You call Bruce Lee sissy? He humtum you good, hah!"

Mrs. Lee was glaring at them. "Enough talking English, already! Speak Mandarin!"

Today was Tuesday, which meant Mike had to report to the office after lunch for his weekly interrogation session with Miss Kumar. *The Boy's*

Book of Spy Craft didn't have a chapter on resisting torture, but if it did, Mike was sure, it would have stressed the importance of being prepared. Which was why, when he arrived several minutes late at Miss Kumar's door, he was balancing a cup of tea in both hands.

"Mike. My goodness!"

"I knew you liked tea," said Mike.

The cup was shaking hysterically in its saucer, lukewarm tea splashing over the rim. For a second Mike feared the cup might jump out of his hands and splatter Miss Kumar's sari.

"Let me," said Miss Kumar, taking the cup and saucer from him. The clattering stopped. "This is very thoughtful of you, Mike. But I have to ask. Is this your way of buttering me up?"

Mike sank into the chair facing Miss Kumar's desk. *Name, rank, and serial number.* He would give away as little as he could.

"Well, consider me completely buttered!" Miss Kumar smiled at him as she sat down behind her cluttered desk. She took a long sip of tea and didn't make a face or complain that it was cold.

"I thought today we'd try something different," she said.

Mike tensed. He wasn't prepared for an alteration in the routine.

"Instead of *me* asking all the questions, today we'll let *you* ask the questions. How does that sound?"

The deviousness of the maneuver chilled him. He sat up straight in his chair, digging his fingers into the flesh above his knees. "Questions? About what?"

Miss Kumar smiled, performed an elaborate shrug. "Anything you like!"

Mike frowned, trying to think of a question that wouldn't give too much away.

"There's only one rule," said Miss Kumar, sipping her lukewarm tea. "It has to be a question you really want to know the answer to."

Mike's eyes darted around the office in a panic, looking for some mysterious clue that might prompt a question. He found it sitting there in front of him, right on Miss Kumar's face.

"Why do you have a red dot painted on your forehead?" he asked, and immediately regretted it. The question was too personal.

But Miss Kumar smiled. "That's my *bindi*. It represents what we Hindus call the 'Third Eye' —perception beyond ordinary sight. It's a gateway of sorts, into an inner world…"

"You mean like Extra Sensory Perception?"

Miss Kumar chuckled. "Not quite as spooky as that. It only leads to where God lives in us. I'm sure you Christians have something similar."

"Oh," said Mike. He felt sorry that Miss Kumar was going to Hell. It didn't seem fair.

"Next one!" said Miss Kumar brightly, like a child enjoying a game of twenty questions.

Mike glanced at the clock. How much longer was the ordeal going to last? It was only a matter of time before he slipped up and asked a question that would give away too much and expose him for what he was. He needed to create a smokescreen. He needed one big question that would keep Miss Kumar's mind occupied for the remainder of their time. A question so interesting and psychological that her school-counselor brain couldn't resist.

"Actually, I *do* have a question," said Mike.

Miss Kumar rubbed her palms together in exaggerated suspense. "Ask me!"

"How do you make friends with someone who doesn't want to be your friend?"

At first Miss Kumar seemed taken aback. It took a while for her smile to return. "A very good question," she said, tilting her head as she pondered. "I think the short answer is, you can't."

For a second, Mike felt outmaneuvered. Miss Kumar had seen through his smokescreen question and counterattacked with the short answer trick. But then she added: "That's the nature of friendship, isn't it. That it's voluntary. If you try to make someone be your friend, then it all falls apart."

"So you should just give up?"

Miss Kumar seemed to be looking at him with all three of her eyes. "Perhaps not give up," she said. "But let go. Give the person the freedom to make up her own mind."

Mike blushed.

"Oh," said Miss Kumar, zeroing in with lasers on full blast. "I assumed it was a *girl* you were talking about. But it's not, is it?"

Mike slid lower in his chair. He wished he could make himself small enough to disappear.

But Miss Kumar seemed relieved. "Well, let's look at the bigger picture. Maybe there's an interest you share with this boy, some kind of activity. That's often how friendships come about. Spending time with someone, doing something you like…"

Chapter 14

On Friday, dozens of American kids showed up at the hostel, carrying Bibles and wearing their best faded jeans. Some arrived on foot, others came in taxicabs, or their parents drove them in air-conditioned cars. As usual, Patrick was one of the first to arrive.

"Greetings, earthling," said Patrick in a reedy voice, flashing a Vulcan salute. He carried a Good News Bible with a blue-jean cover, and highlighter pens in three different colors in his shirt pocket. "We better hurry up, or we'll be late," he said.

Shep had started strumming his guitar, and the assembly room was filling up with teenagers. Kids squeezed shoulder-to-shoulder into rattan sofas and chairs, or sprawled on the floor. Mike and Patrick found an empty spot on the rug and sat with their legs crisscrossed.

Pastor Bob presided over Bible study from the velvet armchair where Mrs. Watkins usually sat. He pointed his beard around the room, smiling. Shep began to play his guitar for real, finger-picking a melody they all knew by heart. Voices joined in, one or two at a time, until pretty soon everybody was singing. The song never failed to fill Mike with sadness, though not in a bad way, because it told how Jesus was coming back, and all the Christians were going to get sucked up into Heaven. Only the unsaved people would be left behind.

After the song, there was a prayer. Then everybody got out their Bibles and started flipping through pages. Pastor Bob called on a tall girl to read tonight's verses out loud.

"For whosoever shall call upon the name of the Lord shall be saved," the girl read in a trembly voice.

Pastor Bob raised his finger in the air. "For *whosoever*—hold on to those words a minute now—whosoever shall call upon the name of the

Lord *shall* be saved. So according to Paul, who is salvation *for?* Is it only for good people?"

"No!" the kids chorused back.

"Is it only for Americans?"

"No!"

"Only for Dallas Cowboys fans?"

Laughter. "No!"

"Who then?

"Anybody!" a kid called out.

Pastor Bob cupped a hand to his ear in mock surprise. "Did you say just *anybody?*"

"Anybody who accepts Jesus as their savior."

"Ah." Pastor Bob held up his finger again. "Now we're getting to the heart of it. But here's a question for you. What if you've never even *heard* of Jesus? How can you accept a savior you don't know?" Pastor Bob let the question hang in the air. Nobody knew how to answer it. Mike stared at his Bata sneakers as the silence seemed to eat up all the oxygen in the room. Pastor Bob said, "Jennifer, can you read the next verse, please?"

The girl picked up her Bible again. She smiled nervously at Pastor Bob, her face flushed from the attention. But this time her voice was less shaky as she read: *"How then shall they call on him in whom they have not believed? and how shall they believe in him of whom they have not heard?"*

Pastor Bob nodded his head, looking around the room until his eyes had brushed each one of them in turn. "How shall they believe in him of whom they have not heard?"

Nobody had an answer. The room grew so quiet, Mike could hear the faint hum of the fluorescent lightbulb on the ceiling. He felt a need to jump up and down and scream. But luckily, he didn't have to, because Patrick raised his hand. "*We* have to tell them," said Patrick. "Or they won't be saved."

Pastor Bob nodded, pointing out the middle-school kid whose wisdom had put the rest of them to shame. Patrick beamed. But the preacher's face was dead serious. "The question now is, what are we

54

going to do about it?" Pastor Bob looked around the room again, from boy to girl to boy, holding each of them, one by one, in his gaze. "What are *you* going to do?"

Mike felt responsible as he thought of all the people he hadn't told about Jesus. People who were going to Hell because he was too much of a coward to tell them the Truth. People like Miss Kumar with her painted-on extra eye. Or Jin Kim, believing all the wrong things he'd been taught.

Nobody else was going to help Jin Kim. Mike was his only hope, and he wasn't leaving anything to chance. He brought his Bible with him to lunch and prayed extra hard while he waited in line.

"Can I hepch you?" said Mr. Ho from behind the counter.

Mike opened his eyes as somebody pushed him from behind.

"*Nasi goreng*, please," he said.

Mike carried his fried rice and Coke on a meandering path between tables, keeping Jin Kim in his line of vision. It wasn't hard. Jin Kim was digging into his fried noodles with a pair of chopsticks, head bent down over the bowl, a fringe of hair falling across his bright dark eyes. A comic book lay open on the table in front of him.

Mike felt light-headed as he got closer, the tray wobbling in his hands. "Hey man," his voice squeaked. "Okay if I sit here?" It didn't come out anything like he had rehearsed.

The chopsticks stopped moving. For a second, when he looked up, Jin Kim seemed caught off guard. Then his face slackened, as if boredom were a mask he could put on or take off. He shrugged. "Free country, lah. Anyhow, I almost finish already."

Mike slid his tray onto the table and sat on the bench across from him. He poked at his fried rice with his fork. "What you reading?"

Jin Kim rolled his eyes and flicked the page over. "Captain America. Very stupid one."

The silence between them seemed to grow. Jin Kim went back to reading his comic book, and Mike decided he would read, too. He lifted the New Testament from his lap and opened it to the Gospel of John. In the corner of his eye, he saw Jin Kim look up.

"Bible, is it? You Jesus Freak or what?"

"No."

Jin Kim wrinkled his nose. "What for you bring to school?"

Mike shrugged. "It's for Language Arts. I needed something to read." But he winced inwardly at his own cowardice—why couldn't he just tell the truth? *And the cock crew...*

"*Sian*, man. Enough boring books already. Social study, Engrish, all make me want sleep."

"But the Bible isn't—"

Jin Kim lifted a small stack of comics off the bench next to him. "Can borrow you one if want. Got Spiderman, Batman. Incredible Hulk also can. Later we trade, okay?"

Before Mike knew what he was doing, his hand reached for the Incredible Hulk. As soon his fingers touched the comic's pulpy spine, he realized what he had done. *And the cock crew a second time.*

"But I don't have one to trade," Mike said.

"Neh mind." Jin Kim leaned forward on his elbows, sliding his open *Captain America* toward Mike. "Look, man." He flipped the pages quickly until he came to the classified ads in the back, then pressed his fingertip onto the glossy page.

"X-ray glasses?"

"Yeah man," said Jin Kim. "For look at *chio bu*. That solid or what?"

Mike shrugged. "It's probably a rip-off."

Jin Kim scowled. "How you know?"

"Besides," said Mike, "it wouldn't be right."

"Eh?"

"Looking at girls with x-ray glasses. Even if you could."

"Relak, man! I only joking lah! You *macam ayam* like my old auntie."

"I'm just saying," said Mike. He hadn't meant to start an argument. Jin Kim was frowning at him, his one chance at salvation slipping away, all because Mike didn't have enough courage. *Before the cock crow twice, thou shalt deny me thrice.* He had denied Jesus when the Lord most needed him, and now everything was falling apart. "Besides," he blurted, blood rushing to his face, "the Bible isn't boring. It's how you get saved."

"Eh? Saved from what?"

There was no going back now. "I mean, accepting Christ as your savior," Mike said in a trembly voice. "So you can go to Heaven."

"*Ang moh*, you need relak, lah. Many lives yet before Heaven."

"I just don't want you to go to Hell, that's all."

Jin Kim scowled. "*Wah piang* eh! In next life, you be cockroach!"

"I can pray with you now, if you want."

"Go fly kite, man!" Jin Kim shoved his tray against Mike's, and the plate of fried rice flipped onto his lap.

"Hey!" Mike jumped up, his crotch stained with grease and soy sauce. Jin Kim laughed.

The next thing that happened was an accident. Without being told by his brain, Mike's arm swept across the table, and Jin Kim's noodles went flying. Bowl and chopsticks bounced off the pagan boy's chest and clattered on the floor. Jin Kim looked down at his stained white shirt, then back at Mike. The usually noisy cafeteria had gone quiet. Then there was a sound, like a half-human growl, building in Jin Kim's throat. "*Kiam pah*, ah!"

Jin Kim lunged, arms extended like battering rams, and both boys hit the ground wrestling. The cafeteria broke into pandemonium as a mob of kids encircled them, chanting, "Fight! Fight!"

But instead of hitting each other, they mostly rolled around on the floor. Scraps of fried rice invaded their hair. Noodles attached to their skin like leeches.

Seconds later, Mike felt himself being lifted by his shirt collar.

Mr. Ho held them apart like dangling marionettes, as the crowd hooted and howled. "You so bad ones!" he said. "Mr. Ho's cuisine for joying, not for fighting!"

Chapter 15

"Damn, Mikey," said Krisda. "You got in a fight?"

"Wild man!" said Bryan.

During Study Hour his roommates took turns looking at him and snorting with laughter. Later, the high-schoolers paraded in to inspect his wounds and offer advice. Mike was a celebrity.

"So, who won?" Shep wanted to know. "Did you get some good licks in, at least?"

Mike shrugged, sitting on the edge of his bed, feeling uncomfortable with all the attention. "Not really."

"Wait. You didn't hit him back?"

"No," said Mike. "I didn't want to hurt him."

Shep sidled next to him on the bed and touched the scratch on his cheek lightly with his finger. "I guess that was Christian of you," he said. "But Mike?"

"What?"

"I don't think the Lord would've minded if you got in a lick or two."

Mike's notoriety even spread to the staff quarters, where his name could be heard in conversation among the amahs and cooks. Getchu ambushed him after dinner with a wooden spoon. "My boys not fighting," she said, shaking the spoon at him. "My boys study! Can behave yourself or not?"

"Okay, okay!"

"Can or not?"

"Can!"

But Mrs. Watkins was less than impressed. She did not appreciate being summoned to school for a talk with the counselor. Mike cringed in his chair as she and Miss Kumar took turns with the tongue-lashing.

The suspension would be in-school, it was decided. He didn't remember anything else of what they said.

On the van ride next morning, he felt strangely apart from the boisterous children around him. He wore his school uniform like always, but he had no books in his lap to anchor him.

"Have a nice day," said Krisda, when they arrived at school.

"Yeah, have fun cleaning toilets," said Bryan, turning to follow the crowd.

Mike stood for a minute on the pavement next to the van, his arms unbearably light at his sides, watching as kids spilled out of cars and buses to join the stream of humanity he was no longer a part of. Nothing felt real.

The custodian's office was on the other side of campus, between the gym and the playing fields. When Mike got there, his enemy was already waiting outside the door. The boys did not look at each other or talk to each other. Mike staked out a piece of wall and leaned against it, taking up the same guilty pose as Jin Kim—hands in pockets, looking down at his sneakers. This is how Mr. Omar found them when he emerged from the storage room with a bucket and two mops.

The boys straightened up. "*Salamat pagi*," they said, almost in unison. Mr. Omar was to be their jailor for the day, so it behooved them to be polite. Mike had expected a scolding, but Mr. Omar returned their greeting with a nod. He said nothing of their crime.

Mr. Omar gave each boy a mop, then picked up the heavy bucket and led them, with small quick steps, along the tiled walkway. A minute later they were in Mr. Ho's open-air cafeteria. A clatter of activity echoed from the kitchen, but the seating area was empty.

"You mop," said Mr. Omar, gesturing at the floor.

The floor did not seem dirty to Mike, but he guessed that was the point. Cleaning a dirty floor would have made sense. It would have conferred on them a dignity they did not deserve.

Mr. Omar showed them how to dip the mop and wring it out. He showed them how to sweep the mop head across the tiles, using a figure-eight motion. When it was Mike's turn to try, he almost tipped

59

over the bucket. "*Ang moh*, you so *kayu!*" Jim Kim grabbed the edge of the bucket to steady it. "What, you never did before?"

Mike didn't say anything. He didn't want to give his enemy one more thing to hold over him. He took his mop and began sweeping the way Mr. Omar had showed them, and before long he had lost himself in the swirling motion of the mop-hairs. It must have been several minutes later when he looked up, and the custodian was gone. Mr. Omar had deserted them.

Mike was shocked. How could adults be so trusting? Now he would have to face his enemy alone.

As if sensing the danger too, Jin Kim kept his distance, and the boys started on opposite sides of the cafeteria. As they worked toward the middle, Mike mopped carefully, going over the same tiles again and again, until his arms ached. But no matter how slowly he worked, they were sure to meet in the middle at some point, and then what? Already they were that much nearer to each other, the hairs of their swirling mop heads close enough to tangle.

Finally, the mop heads collided at the exact place where they had been sitting yesterday, the moment before catastrophe had struck. It was a moment that existed now only in a parallel universe—the universe in which Mike and Jim Kim had become friends.

Still the boys did not look at each other.

"What are we supposed to do now?" said Mike. He looked around for an adult but didn't find one.

"We finish already."

"But it's only second period."

Jim Kim nodded uneasily. "This school got no proper rules, everything *bo cheng hu!* Where Mr. Omar go, ah? He fly aeroplane!"

"Maybe we should keep mopping. Just in case."

Jin Kim nodded. "Up there," he said, pointing to the walkway.

This time they worked side by side, pushing their mops in front of them, hoping an adult would come by and notice them. But nobody came except a sick fourth-grader clutching a hall pass, on his way to the nurse.

After a while they gave up all pretense of cleaning, and instead raced each other up and down the walkway, pushing their mops like hockey sticks. Jin Kim found a paper cup to use as a puck, and they made a game of it. But even that got boring after a while. Third period came and went, and they were still unsupervised.

"Maybe they forgot us," said Mike, leaning against the wall. Above his head, a bulletin board screamed *BE A SUPER-STAR!* in big shiny letters.

Jin Kim rested his chin on his mop handle and studied the poster. "Look, *ang moh*. This one for you. *Jesus Freak Superstar!*"

Mike scowled. "That's so funny I forgot to laugh." But he followed Jin Kim's gaze to the bulletin board, where a half-empty sign-up sheet hung from a bent staple.

"Why you not sign up?" said Jim Kim. "Too scared?"

"For your information," said Mike crisply, "I *did* sign up. We have bulletin boards in Beta, too, you know."

"Really? Solid siah!" Jin Kim held his mop handle like a microphone and started crooning the words to "Superstar."

Mike tried to keep a straight face, but it didn't work. Jin Kim singing into his mop handle, swinging his narrow hips like Elvis—the dementedness was infectious, and soon Mike was strumming his mop like a guitar, nodding his head to the beat, making twanging sounds with his voice to keep time. At just the right moment, his guitar turned into a microphone, and they both joined in for the chorus, singing so loud and shameless their voices rang against the walls. They hadn't yet noticed the crowd gathering outside Mr. Ho's kitchen.

Mike saw them first, and froze. For a few seconds more Jin Kim cavorted in song, eyes closed in concentration. Then he saw them, too, and took a sharp breath, planting his mop handle on the floor.

A gathering of janitors and cooks stood watching them. Some of them were frowning, others seemed perplexed. Mr. Omar's face showed no emotion at all.

Then the applause came, rows of faces lighting up with smiles, and there was only one thing they could do. Side by side, they turned to their audience and bowed.

Chapter 16

As it turned out, Mike and Jin Kim were not the only boys who showed up for auditions. Others came too, slinking in secretly like fugitives. The auditorium was shaped like an amphitheater with carpeted tiers descending to a small stage, and all the boys gravitated toward the back—which was where Jin Kim found Mike, sitting in the shadows where he could blend in with the wall.

"*Ang moh*, you came! You not *ayam?*" He flapped his arms and made clucking noises.

"Wow, you're hilarious. By the way, I do have a name, you know."

Jin Kim plonked himself down on the floor next to him. "Relak, Mike. Only joking lah."

There was an enthusiastic buzz all around them, and Mike couldn't help being infected by the excitement, despite his best efforts to stay alert. A man in a flowery shirt came out on stage and clapped his hands together. "Oh, my goodness," said Mr. Jenkins, looking up and down the tiers in exaggerated awe. "Look at all these stars. They're all so *beautiful!*"

There were groans from the boys in the back, but Mr. Jenkins ignored them. "What do you reckon, Mr. Stone, are they beautiful?"

"Beautiful!" agreed Mr. Stone, tinkling a few notes on the piano.

"Groovy. Alright, everybody up!" Mr. Jenkins clapped his hands again, shooing kids to their feet. "And sing along with me!"

Mr. Stone joined in on the piano, and a few kids sang along timidly. Mr. Jenkins made a horrified face, until the hesitant singing dissolved into giggles.

"This isn't a *dirge*, guys," said Mr. Jenkins, waving everyone quiet. "You're not in church singing some godawful hymn. This is a *joyful* song, alright? It's Jesus' triumphant entry! So let's hear some joy! Pick up your palm leaves and wave them around. That's it!"

Mr. Stone played the intro again, and the chorus joined in louder and more upbeat. Everyone was singing this time.

Mike lost himself in the song, waving his imaginary palm fronds like Mr. Jenkins was doing on stage. The teacher was swaying from side to side like a demented palm tree, and it was hard not to laugh, but harder still not to join in. Everyone was getting into it now.

Mike stole a sideways glance and caught Jin Kim's eye. They were both grinning.

At the warehouse later that day, Mike reported the grin to Mr. Keen.

"That's good," said Mr. Keen. "That's very good."

The Tae Kwon Do sessions after school were becoming more and more brutal. Mr. Keen and Mr. Wong took turns putting him through the wringer. They paired him with the most vicious boys as sparring partners. They made him stretch his limbs into impossible contortions, forced him to walk in a squatting position until his knees screamed. They made him practice kicks and punches and blocks in endless combinations, repeated over and over. If he messed up, he was punished. The slightest inattention could earn him another twenty pushups on his knuckles or fingertips. His hands had become hard and calloused, his body a patchwork of bruises. Still, every session began with a bow and ended with a bow. Mr. Keen was pleased.

"You're becoming a tough little fighter," he said after class. "Wong thinks you're ready for the next level, and I have to agree."

Mike savored the moment, though Mr. Keen seemed distracted. Class had been over for a while, and Mike had already changed back into his school clothes, but they still hadn't left the warehouse. Mr. Keen had his attaché case open on the desk in the little office.

"So what happens now?" said Mike.

Mr. Keen didn't answer, lost in whatever he was reading.

"Mr. Keen?"

"Hmm?"

Mike opened the mini-fridge in the corner and got himself a Coke, hoping the violation of protocol would get Mr. Keen's attention. When that didn't work, he turned on the portable radio that rested on the desk. An Elvis Presley song blared from the tinny little speaker.

"Turn it down," Mr. Keen said crossly, but he didn't look up from his paperwork. Neither did he say anything about Mike pilfering a Coke from the fridge—a theft the American taxpayer would have to pay for.

Mike took his Coke back into the changing room and practiced his side kicks between sips, slamming his imaginary opponents into the walls. That made him hot and sweaty again, so he took his shirt off.

"Who's Charlie?" said Mr. Keen.

"What?" Mike went back to the office and poked his head in.

Mr. Keen held up the letter he was reading. The light from the desk lamp made the thin paper glow. Even from this far away Mike recognized the swirling loops of his mother's handwriting. "Your mother says to take care of Charlie. Who's Charlie?"

Mike was instantly wary. "I don't know," he said. Cola bubbles burned the back of his throat. He burped.

Mr. Keen's sharp blue eyes looked like they might cut him in half. "Mike. What did we discuss the last time?"

Mike leaned his back against the doorjamb, letting his sneakers slide out in front of him. "Tell you everything."

"So who," said Mr. Keen, shaking the paper in his hand, "is Charlie?"

Mike jumped into a fighting stance and hammered the air with a rapid-fire series of punches.

"Mike!"

"It's a stupid stuffed animal, okay?" He spun out the office door, back into the changing room, and front-kicked somebody's uniform off its hook. "Charlie the tiger. I had him when I was little."

"Oh." Mr. Keen let out a breath. He seemed disappointed.

Mike found his bottle of Coke where he had left it on the bench and took a big slurp. Then he remembered there was something else he wanted to ask. He came back into the office and watched as Mr. Keen

64

folded the paper carefully and put it back in its envelope. "When can I have my letters back?"

"These letters are classified until further notice."

"You mean I can't read an old letter from my mom because it's Top Secret?"

Mike folded his arms and waited for Mr. Keen to say something about his smart-assed attitude. He was pressing his luck in a way his dad would never let him get away with. But Mr. Keen was quiet as he closed the lid of his attaché case. Which was another big difference between Mr. Keen and Mike's father—Dad carried an old-fashioned lawyer's briefcase that opened from the top. It had a sweaty, leathery man-smell Mike remembered from those few occasions when he had found it unlocked.

"Is there anything you haven't told me, Mike?"

"No, sir."

"Anything your parents might have sent you? Anything they might have said to you?"

Mike sighed impatiently. "Can we go now? I'll miss dinner. It's spaghetti tonight."

Mr. Keen gave Mike a long look, as if trying to decide how much the boy could be trusted. He lifted the Coke bottle out of Mike's hand and set it on the desk. "You understand your instructions for this week?"

"Yes, sir."

"Put your shirt on. We'll go over it again in the car."

Chapter 17

Wake up. Breakfast. Van ride. School. Tae Kwon Do. Dinner. Devotions. Homework. Free time. Shower. Bed.

This was Mike's life most days. And yet underneath the routine, there was a whole other life, too. A secret life he could tell no one about. Especially not Miss Kumar, whose weekly interrogation sessions had so far failed to break him. Even if he *did* give in and confess, she might not believe him. She might even think he was crazy and send him to the nurse to get tranquilized. It was hard, not being able to tell anyone.

Oddly, the person he most wanted to tell was Jin Kim. They were hanging out more lately—not just in Mandarin class and drama club, but even during their free time. In the cafeteria they traded comic books, haggling between mouthfuls of fried rice.

"Wah, *Amazing Spiderman!*" said Jin Kim, grabbing greedily. "Like new, this one. Where buy?"

Mike hedged. "I forget." He couldn't tell Jin Kim the truth—that all his comics came from the news stand in the lobby of the Shangri-La Hotel. Mr. Keen had insisted on paying for them. It was a valid business expense, he said.

"Neh mind," said Jin Kim. "I borrow you my Captain America for this one."

"Captain America? No way."

"Can bring Ghost Rider tomorrow. Or Incredible Hulk."

"I read those already."

"*Wah piang* eh! Why you so greedy one?"

"You're trying to rip me off, man."

"Okay, okay," said Jin Kim. "Special deal for you only…" He

darted his eyes around the cafeteria before slipping his fingers into his pocket.

"What is it?" said Mike.

Jin Kim laid a matchbox on the table with gentle care, as if it contained enough TNT to blow up the school. "I show you," he said, beckoning Mike to look closer.

Mike suspected it was a trick, but curiosity overwhelmed common sense. Warily, he pushed his half-finished plate of fried rice aside and huddled closer. Jin Kim's fingers nudged the matchbox open a crack.

A pair of black bulbous eyes stared out at them. "His name Satu," said Jin Kim.

"Dang!" Mike flinched back. "You want to trade a *real* spider for my *Spiderman?* No way!"

"What talking you?" said Jin Kim sourly. "Satu not for sale, lah."

Mike screwed up his face. "Then what—"

"Borrow me *Amazing Spiderman*, and tomorrow I teach you catch spider for ownself."

"What for?" said Mike. "I hate spiders."

"For fighting, man! Satu, he number one champion. Tomorrow we catch number two for you." Jin Kim closed the matchbox. "Special deal for you. Make you hundred-percent Singapore boy, no more *ang moh*. Can or not?"

It was only a business transaction. So why did he feel like he was in free fall? He didn't know what to say. All he could do, finally, was offer Jin Kim his hand. "Can," he said.

"Solid siah!" said Jin Kim, smiling as they shook on it. "Tomorrow we hunt."

Tae Kwon Do. Dinner. Devotions. Homework. Free time. Shower. Bed. Wake up. Get dressed. Breakfast. Van ride.

"Please God," Mike prayed as he stepped off the Volkswagen bus. Today the cast list was going to be posted, and he wanted God to know that it was really okay if he only got a small part, but if he *did* get a bigger part—like, say, the role of Jesus—he would do the best he could.

He found Jin Kim waiting by the bulletin board.

"Not yet," said Jin Kim. "Maybe lunch time."

They both stared at the faint rectangle where the sign-up sheet used to be, now an empty space of terrifying possibility.

"We'll probably get small parts," said Mike.

Jin Kim shrugged. "Neh mind. Is only a play, lah."

"Yeah. No big deal."

They looked at each other.

"You bring it or not?" said Jin Kim.

Mike fished the empty matchbox out of his pocket to show him. "It wasn't easy. I had to borrow it from Austin's desk. He's the only one who smokes." Mike had taken only the box and left the matches, so technically it wasn't stealing.

"Okay," said Jin Kim. "Come let's go."

"What, *now?*"

"Morning best time for spider hunting. Afternoon, spider get sleepy."

They took off through the morning crowd, Mike still clutching his math homework under one arm. He looked at his watch. There were only ten minutes left before homeroom. "Are you sure we have enough time?"

"Teachers not punish us," said Jin Kim. "This school everything *bo cheng hu*. Anyhow, spider more important."

"What's the hurry?" said Mike, jogging to keep up. "I already gave you *Amazing Spiderman!*"

Jin Kim barely shrugged in answer. He was on some kind of mission, it seemed to Mike, and it was about more than just comics or spiders. They waved to Mr. Omar as they passed the custodian's office, then broke into a run across the playing fields toward a patch of jungle on the other side.

"We look for jumping spider, like Satu," Jin Kim whispered. In the stillness, every sound was amplified—every word, every cracking twig, every grass blade whisking against their legs. Time melted away, and Mike stopped looking at his watch. He left his math books in a pile and followed Jin Kim deeper into the forest. They crouched beneath a tangle of trees. Jim Kim reached for a leaf and gently turned it over in his hand. Dappling sunlight played on his face. "Not this one," he said as a small spider scurried up the branch. "Need boy spider only."

"How do you know if it's a boy?"

"Boys more blue color," said Jin Kim. "Like this one!" He cupped a leaf in both hands.

Mike recoiled. He hadn't expected to have to touch it.

"Pull your shirt out," said Jin Kim. "Make like basket."

Mike lifted his shirttail, and Jin Kim flung open his hands. The spider scurried up the front of Mike's shirt, stopped on a button to rest. A small dark creature with bulging eyes and bright blue stripes on its legs. Mike opened the matchbox and gently coaxed the spider inside, where a leafy bed and a fruit-fly supper was waiting for him.

"Steady lah!" said Jin Kim, grinning. "Got champion one!"

"Solid siah!" said Mike, grinning back.

For a while they knelt in the undergrowth, knees pressing into a brittle carpet of leaves. Mike held the matchbox in both hands. Sunlight flickered through the canopy, playing on their faces like a secret festival of lights. Until a thin green snake nosed its way through the parting grass, and they knew it was time to go.

They didn't run, even though they were more than ten minutes late. Mike held the matchbox in front of him as they emerged from the jungle and crossed the playing field.

"I'll call him Peter," said Mike. "That's Spiderman's real name."

"Good one ah!"

They paused at the bulletin board before parting ways.

"Better put Peter in pocket," said Jin Kim. "Don't want teachers make trouble."

Mike nodded. He cringed a little as he slipped the matchbox into his pocket. But Peter would be safe there, as long as he didn't make any sudden moves.

When Mike got to class, Mr. Stone was already writing equations on the blackboard.

"Good *afternoon*, Mike, so good of you to join us!"

Laughter. Kids were turning in their seats to smirk at him. But

Mike didn't care. He dipped his hand into his pocket and felt the matchbox with his fingers.

"What's the excuse, Mike?" said Mr. Stone, throwing his piece of chalk up in the air and catching it again. "Go on, let's hear it. Miss the bus? Catching up on beauty sleep?"

More laughter. Mike reddened. He had seen this game played out before, and Mr. Stone always won. But he remembered what *The Boy's Book of Spy Craft* said: sometimes, a secret agent's best defense is the truth.

"I was hunting spiders in the jungle," he said.

Mr. Stone did a comic double take, then stared at Mike in exaggerated disbelief. His audience dissolved into giggling fits. "Did you catch any?"

"Yes, sir," said Mike, fishing the matchbox out of his pocket.

The laughter subsided. Kids were sitting up in their seats, peering with bemused interest.

"It's a jumping spider," said Mike. "For fighting other spiders."

A hush fell over the room. Then there were gasps. "But that's horrible!" said a girl. "So cruel!" said someone else. "You should let it go!"

"But they *like* to fight!" Mike protested. "Anyway, it's a Singapore thing. All the kids do it."

Mr. Stone cleared his throat. "Well, let's leave it in its box for now, shall we."

Nervous laughter.

Mike slipped the matchbox back into his pocket. He stood, waiting to be invited to sit down, digging at the carpet with the toe of his sneaker.

"And where's your homework, Mike?" Mr. Stone raised an eyebrow. "Or did you leave it in the jungle?"

"Um—"

Mr. Stone rolled his eyes, and the class erupted in hysterics. "I think Mike wins first prize, what do you reckon, guys?"

Cheers. Scattered applause.

Mike slid into a chair near the back and did his best to disappear. Jin Kim was right about one thing—this school was *bo cheng hu*.

Chapter 18

All through morning classes, Mike's nerves were out of control. His right leg was jumping up and down like it wanted to shake itself loose. He worried about Peter imprisoned in his pocket, and pressed down on his knee to stop the shaking. But that meant he didn't have a free hand to write with, which made Mrs. Holmes suspicious that he was daydreaming again.

"Those sentences aren't going to diagram themselves, Mike," said Mrs. Holmes, sidling up to his desk.

"I'm thinking."

Mrs. Holmes raised an eyebrow, but left him alone.

Mike kept his eyes on the clock on the wall, and as soon as the two hands met at the 12, he was up out of his seat and running.

"Mike!" the teacher called after him, but he was already gone.

He barreled through the double glass doors of the Learning Community and skidded around the corner. Unbelievably, a small crowd had already gathered at the bulletin board, and he had to jostle his way to the front. Jin Kim was staring fixedly at the empty space where the cast list was supposed to be. "Not yet," he said.

"Dang! They're torturing us on purpose!"

They waited, sweating in the humid shade. Some kids got bored and wandered off to the cafeteria. Then they heard the singing.

It came from far away, at first. Not kids' voices, but deep men's voices. The singing got louder and nearer, until Mr. Jenkins and Mr. Stone rounded the corner like a procession of rowdy choirboys. Mr. Jenkins waved a piece of paper like a palm branch as they made their triumphant entry. The spectacle was so stupid, Mike couldn't stop himself grinning.

"*Bo cheng hu,*" said Jin Kim, shaking his head.

"All right, you stars," said Mr. Jenkins. "We've assigned all the parts, and it was *really* difficult, wasn't it, Mr. Stone?"

"*Bloody* difficult, Mr. Jenkins!"

"Because you're all so beautiful and brilliant!" Mr. Jenkins shook the paper in his hand to emphasize how great they all were. "So just remember, there's *no such thing* as a small part! Because every part is *absolutely essential!*"

"Too right, Mr. Jenkins!" said Mr. Stone. "And we're counting on every of one you to work flat out to make the show a success."

Mike wished they would stop talking and post the list already. By the looks of him, Jin Kim was feeling the same.

"Without further ado," said Mr. Jenkins, giving the paper a final flourish.

The crowd pressed in closer.

"We don't say 'good luck' in show business," said Mr. Stone. "What do we say, guys?"

Eye-rolls. Groans. "Break a leg," everyone murmured lackadaisically.

"I didn't hear that, did you, Mr. Jenkins?"

"Didn't hear a thing, Mr. Stone."

The cast sighed in unison, gathered its breath to roar, "Break a leg!"

"*That's* more like it!"

The moment finally came. Mr. Stone ceremonially handed Mr. Jenkins a thumbtack, and Mr. Jenkins, with exaggerated formality, pinned the paper to the board.

A minute later Mike was running. He needed to get out of there fast, because he was going to cry. Already a sob was building in the back of his throat, and the floodgates behind his eyes were on the brink of bursting.

He dashed into the boys' room and locked himself into the farthest stall. He perched atop the toilet seat, drew his knees up in a tight hug, and quietly bawled. He cried as boys came and went. A urinal flushed, and he cried. Water splashed in the sink as someone washed his hands, and he cried some more. He wept painfully, with huge wracking sobs, until his knees were wet with tears. He would stay here in this toilet stall forever until he died.

After a while the urinals stopped flushing and the sinks went silent. The only sound was Mike's shaky breathing. The boys' room door swung open again. A blast of lunch time noise, then quiet. This time the footsteps were heavier, hard shoes knocking on the tiles. A pair of grown-up loafers appeared below the stall door.

"Mike? You right, mate?"

Mike sniveled. He hugged his knees tighter as another sob wracked his body.

"It's alright, you can come out," said Mr. Stone. "Mr. Jenkins is standing guard outside. It's just you and me."

"Leave me alone!"

There was a sigh from the other side of the stall door. "We thought you'd be *thrilled*. Honestly. It's a starring role."

"You made me the *bad* guy!"

"Not *all* bad," said Mr. Stone patiently. "He's a complicated character, don't you think?"

Mike found a pen in his shirt pocket and decided he was going to write some graffiti. He bit the cap off with his teeth and scratched ink into the wall.

"I mean, he *loves* Jesus, right? But he sees his friend growing away from him. He wants to protect him, protect what they have together…"

"He's a traitor!" said Mike, digging deeper into the plaster with his pen.

"That's the irony, isn't it? But in a way, he only does what he *has* to do. It's all foretold, you see? Without a crucifixion, there's no resurrection. Without Judas, no Christ."

Mike looked at what he had written. JUDAS + JESUS. He started to draw a circle around it.

"Bottom line, Mike, is we *need* you. Without Judas, we haven't got a play. Besides, you and Jin Kim are *dynamite* together! There's a connection between you two that's *electric*. The audience isn't gonna know what hit 'em!"

Mike shaped the circle into a heart around the names. He jumped off the toilet seat and slid open the latch on the door.

Mr. Stone was beaming down on him like a sunshower of gentle rain. "What do we say in show business?"

Mike wiped his nose on his sleeve. "Break a leg?"

"Too right, mate!" The teacher ruffled Mike's hair and pried, from Judas' tear-stained face, a smile.

Chapter 19

Through the fog of his dream, a far-off clanging. Getchu was ringing the breakfast bell. But when Mike opened his eyes, the light in the room seemed somehow wrong—too bright for wakeup time—and his roommates still lay in twisted heaps. It must be Saturday.

A day of freedom. A whole day of nobody telling him what to do.

His sarong fell to his ankles as he stepped out of bed. From his dresser drawer he picked out a pair of cutoff jeans and his favorite Oklahoma Sooners T-shirt—which was faded and a little frayed along the neckline, but it would have to do. He needed an especially American outfit to help him get past the Marine guards. Because today he had business at the Embassy of the United States.

The bus was more crowded for a Saturday than he expected—whole families out for a day in town, with old aunties and uncles along for the ride, yammering in a babel of languages. The only spare seat was next to an old lady who held a live chicken on her lap. Mike greeted her in Mandarin, and she answered cheerfully with a flood of Hokkien. The bound chicken flapped its wings pitifully and stared at him with an accusing eye. Mike had to perch on the edge of the seat to keep his bare legs out of range of its claws.

The city floated past—cluttered shophouses and outdoor stalls gave way to neatly trimmed streets and official looking buildings. Mike got off at Bras Basah Road, glad to put some distance between himself and the chicken. He walked the last few blocks to the embassy.

A blast of air conditioning chilled him as he entered through the glass doors. Immediately he was aware of being watched. A hundred pairs of eyes took turns stealing curious glances. Being a kid on his

75

own made him conspicuous, and he considered finding an adult to tag along behind. But *The Boy's Book of Spy Craft* warned against making your cover too complicated. Sometimes, hiding in plain sight was the best of bad options.

The foyer was busy, but not crowded. There was a line of people waiting for visas, and another line waiting at the information window. Between the two lines, a young marine stood guard at a nondescript door.

Mike walked up to the marine. "Hi," he said.

The marine flicked his eyes down at Mike but didn't smile. He wasn't much older than nineteen, but he towered over Mike. His muscles seemed to want to bust out of his uniform.

"I guess you're American, huh?" asked Mike.

The marine answered with a blank stare.

"I'm American, too. See?" Mike tugged on his T-shirt to show the Oklahoma Sooners logo.

The marine narrowed his eyes. "Sooner trash, huh?"

Mike was thrown off guard, but adjusted quickly. He made his voice sound like Grandpa's back in the States. "I smell bullshit. Must be some Texas Longhorns around."

A ghost of a smile played on the marine's lips. "Y'all ain't worth spit."

"Sooners are unbeaten," said Mike. "Put that in your pipe and smoke it."

"Even a blind hog can find an acorn once in a while," said the marine.

"That so? Y'all can't win for losing."

"Y'all think the sun shines out of your ass."

"Yeah, well. It's hard to be humble when you're the best."

"Just wait till the Cotton Bowl, buzzard bait!"

"Oh, I'm so scared!"

The marine snorted. "You sure *talk* big, for a little feller. Where's your folks at?"

"That's what I'm here to find out," said Mike. "I need to talk to Colonel West."

For a second, the marine looked confused. "He's top brass around here. What's a kid want with—"

"Please," said Mike. "My parents are in Nam. I haven't got a letter in months."

The marine's tough-guy mask softened. His Adam's apple bobbed in his throat. "Y'all are military?"

Mike's shoulders slumped. "No."

The marine nodded knowingly. "Spooks, then."

Mike kept his lips tightly closed. He had already given away too much.

"Oh, man. You're gonna get me court-martialed."

"Sorry," said Mike.

"Go stand in that line," said the marine, pointing to the information window. "I'll see what help I can scare up. No promises, though."

The line was about six people deep, but Mike wasn't in any hurry to get to the front of it. The official lady behind the plate glass window was scary looking. Right now she was yelling at an old man for letting his green card lapse. Droplets of spit flew from her enraged mouth and hit the window glass. "This is very serious! How could you be so negligent? You may have lost your residency status *permanently!*"

She went on for a few more minutes scolding the old man as she thumped some papers with a rubber stamp. Finally she passed the forms to him through a little drawer under the window and told him to take a seat. The old man hobbled away, shamefaced, like a little boy who'd been slapped.

"Next!" The line shuffled forward a notch.

As he neared the front of the line, Mike started to sweat. His skin stung in the fierce air conditioning. The lady behind the window had begun cussing out somebody's old auntie for filling out a form wrong. Mike was close enough now to see the nose hairs in the official's flared nostrils as she berated the old lady, who didn't seem to understand what she had done wrong.

"Next!" The official's glaring eyes fastened onto Mike. "Where are your parents?" she demanded. "This is no place for unaccompanied *children.*"

Mike had just opened his mouth to speak when he felt a light touch on his arm. He spun around to face a column of shiny gold buttons in a field of Army green. He tilted his head back to peer into the unsmiling face of Colonel Nathaniel West, U.S. Army.

"I thought I made it clear the last time," said the colonel gravely, "that we'll be in touch as soon as we have some news."

"But that was weeks ago," said Mike.

The colonel sighed. "Come on." He steered Mike across the lobby to a row of seats along the wall. They sat down next to a potted tree with rubbery leaves.

"Nobody tells me anything," said Mike, trying to steady the tremble in his voice. "Is anyone even looking for them? What if they got lost, or hurt, or—"

"We're doing everything we can," said the colonel. "But these things take time."

"They're spies, aren't they," Mike blurted. "They're with the CIA or something, that's why you won't tell me anything."

It seemed a full minute before either of them said another word. The air conditioning hummed, and the murmur of voices around them swelled into a soft cocoon.

The colonel studied Mike with a thin-lipped smile. "I understand you're upset, Mike. And you have a vivid imagination. But making up wild stories isn't going to bring them home."

Mike's fingers dug into the flesh around his knees. "You just say that because I'm a kid. I'm not stupid."

The colonel sighed. He laced his fingers together and tucked them under his chin, like a professor in deep thought. Then he seemed to come to a decision and looked levelly at Mike.

"You're a Foreign Service kid, Mike, so you know how this works— at a remote posting like Da Nang, everybody pitches in. Could your dad be involved in some kind of intelligence work?" The colonel shrugged. "*Possibly*. But even if I knew anything, which I don't, that information would be classified. So you're just going to have to trust us."

Mike nodded. He knew Colonel West was taking a risk, talking to him like an adult, and he wanted to show that he could handle it.

But it wasn't enough. "Can't you just tell me," he said, choking on the words. "Are they—"

He was glad at least the colonel didn't try to comfort him, or anything weird like that. Instead, the officer waited for Mike to get control of himself before offering his handkerchief, which Mike refused. He wiped his eyes on his T-shirt and stood up.

"I hear your grandparents have been in touch," the colonel said, slipping the unused handkerchief back in his pocket.

Mike shouldn't have been as surprised as he was. Of course, Mrs. Watkins must have blabbed something to the colonel. The same way *all* the adults had been talking behind his back—Miss Kumar, Mr. Stone, and the rest. Now Colonel West was in on it, too.

"It might be time to take them up on their offer, Mike," said the colonel kindly. "You're not doing anybody any good, hanging around here, pestering embassy officials. Maybe it's time to go back home. Where you belong."

"Belong?" said Mike.

"It's what your parents would have wanted, isn't it?"

Mike shrugged, then nodded dutifully. It wasn't the colonel's fault for being so clueless.

Exiting the embassy's glass doors, the outdoor air felt like a balm, but it didn't stop the shivering. At first he barely noticed the man in the batik shirt and Dodgers baseball cap who was milling around the news stand. But a minute later he caught a glimpse of the man's reflection in the side mirror of a parked taxi, and he knew he was being followed.

Mike picked up his pace and walked straight ahead, too scared to look behind him. He needed to get himself under control, he couldn't afford any more amateurish mistakes. He stopped in the middle of the sidewalk and turned around, dropping to one knee to re-tie his shoe. He took his time with the laces, watching the parade of feet passing by on the edge of his vision. When he glimpsed the Dockers boat shoes approaching, he stood up and looked his pursuer in the eye.

"Don't you ever wear socks?" said Mike.

Jason Keen scowled, but he didn't stop or slow his pace. "Keep walking," he said as he passed. Mike followed, keeping about ten yards between them. He could tell from Mr. Keen's tone that he was in trouble, even though he hadn't done anything wrong.

They passed the Cathedral of the Good Shepherd and continued down Victoria Street. Jason Keen walked at a furious pace, and Mike had to jog every few steps to keep up. They were getting further away from his bus stop and deeper into an unfamiliar part of town. If he got lost, he didn't know how he was going to get home.

They came to a block of shophouses. Mike slowed down as he weaved among the Saturday morning shoppers. The sheltered walkway was cluttered with things for sale, people haggling in Cantonese and Malay and Tamil. Mike bumped his knee on a ceramic jar of hundred-year-old eggs, then collided with a row of roasted ducks dangling from hooks. By the time he regained his balance, Mr. Keen was gone.

In a panic, Mike searched the Chinese grocery, but Mr. Keen wasn't there. He continued on against the press of the crowd, past a tailor shop and an Indian bakery. At the end of the block, he stepped into a busy side street. Someone grabbed his arm.

"What were you doing at the embassy?" Mr. Keen's voice was quiet but urgent, his hand squeezing Mike's arm. He seemed half-crazy, the way his eyes jumped around, the baseball cap slightly askew, his face glistening with sweat.

"You're hurting me," said Mike.

Shoppers were looking at them. Mr. Keen released his grip and put an arm around Mike's shoulders instead. "You and me, we're gonna have a talk," he said, steering Mike through a maze of food stalls. They navigated a hodgepodge of tables set up in the middle of the street, and Mr. Keen pressed Mike down into a chair. "Two *mee goreng*," he said to the vendor as he sat down.

"I don't like *mee goreng*," said Mike.

Mr. Keen's frantic eyes darted left and right before settling again on Mike. "What did you say to the colonel?"

Mike stared. It took him a few seconds more to find his voice. "Mr. Keen, have you been spying on me?"

A few feet away, a wok hissed and steamed as the vendor tossed vegetables into a pool of hot oil. Mr. Keen leveled a finger at Mike. "You've been going around behind my back."

"I have *not!*" said Mike. "You're the one who's sneaking around! Why are you following me?"

"What did you say to the colonel? Did you say anything about me?"

"No!"

"Are you sure?"

"I asked about my parents, okay?" Mike hugged his arms to his chest. "You never tell me anything. I had to find out *somehow.*"

Mr. Keen looked away, silently stewing. Wok grease and exhaust fumes formed a noxious cloud above their heads. Mike fought back the impulse to gag.

"So." Mr. Keen put his sunglasses on. "What did you find out?'

"Nothing. Just the usual crap."

Mr. Keen nodded—a little smugly, it seemed to Mike.

"From now on, any communication with the embassy goes through me. Is that clear?"

"Why?"

"I'm serious, Mike!"

"Okay, jeez!" Mike rolled his eyes. "What's the big deal? I thought you guys were on the same side."

"I need to hear you say it." Mr. Keen leaned forward in his chair. "Say it properly."

The vendor slid two plates onto the table. Mike looked down at his fried noodles and considered throwing the steaming mess into Jason Keen's face. "Yes, sir," he said.

He picked at his *mee goreng* with his chopsticks, separating out the shrimps into a pile of corpses on the edge of his plate. He hated shrimp. He hated *mee goreng*. He hated Jason Keen.

"We're running out of time," Mr. Keen was saying. "We have to start on the next stage of the mission. Even though we're not as ready as I would like us to be."

Mike speared a shrimp on his plate, made a catapult of his chopstick and flicked the tiny carcass into the street.

"There's a journalist, a reporter for *The Straits Times*. He's pursuing a story that we're very interested in. I want you to get close to him, find out what he knows. Maybe get a copy of his notes."

Mike looked up, slack-jawed.

"It could be dangerous," Mr. Keen continued. "We believe this reporter has connections to the communists. We wouldn't ask this of you if it wasn't of the highest importance."

Dangerous. Communists. The words made Mike's face flush, set his heart to pounding. "What reporter?"

Mr. Keen took his sunglasses off and looked straight at him. The panic in his eyes from a moment ago was gone. In its place was something harder, colder. "His name is Chen Jun Ling. Alias, Simon Chen. He uses the English name as his byline." Mr. Keen reached into his shirt pocket for a newspaper clipping and laid it out on the table. The column of print was ten inches long, with a black-and-white picture at the top. Mike noticed something oddly familiar about the man in the photo, but he couldn't tell what it was.

He shook his head. "I've never seen him before. How do I—"

"He has a son, a boy your age…"

Mike watched Mr. Keen's lips form the syllables of a name.

Chapter 20

Mike stood in a maze of food stalls in the chaos of the street, watching Mr. Keen's baseball cap disappear into the Saturday afternoon crowd. He tried to remember the instructions he'd been given, but he couldn't keep anything in his head. He didn't even know where he was, or how he had gotten here, or which way was home.

For a while, Mike weaved his way along the crowded alleyways, stopping at trash cans to hunt Peter's dinner, clapping his hands into swarms of fruit flies. He lost track of time, and day had long turned to night before he finally found his bus stop. On the ride home, he counted the little carcasses he had collected, laying them out in the fold of a paper in his hand.

He walked the lonely road home in darkness, menaced by the shriek of insects and insomniac birds. He had missed dinner, violated his curfew, and was likely in trouble, but he told himself that none of those things mattered as long as the spider was alright. If the spider was alright, then everything else could still be alright. Everything depended upon the small creature alone in its matchbox on the windowsill, without food, without air or light. The spider was the only thing left that was still true.

His sense of urgency grew as he climbed the stairs to the dorm. His roommates were on their way down, and Bryan bumped into him on purpose and said, "Better not go up there."

Mike had to grab the railing to keep from falling. "Why?"

"Austin's on a rampage," said Bryan. "Why did you do it, Mike?"

"Do what?"

"Steal his matches, man! He gets mean when he can't smoke."

"Yeah, *Mike*," said Krisda.

"I didn't steal his matches." Mike shouldered past them up the stairs. "I didn't steal anything."

When he got to their room, he found the matchbox on the windowsill and took it over to his bed. Sitting with legs crossed, he fished the twisted piece of paper out of his pocket and unfolded it. He opened the matchbox carefully, just far enough to drop the fruit flies inside. The spider twitched, and Mike breathed a sigh. "Don't worry, boy. Everything's alright."

"Talking to yourself?"

Mike flinched at the sound of the voice and looked up. Austin was leaning against the door jamb, watching him.

"Oh, hi," said Mike, trying to make his voice sound normal. He uncrossed his legs and swung his feet to the floor. Closed his fingers around the matchbox.

Austin took a few steps further into the room. "Where is it?" He was close enough now that his hands were within slugging distance.

"Where's what?"

The hand swung around in a blur and caught Mike on the right side of the face. The physical force made his head turn. It took a second longer for the pain to come, like a blossoming flame.

"Where's my damn matches?"

"I don't know."

The left hand twitched. Mike anticipated like a nervous goalie, but the blow came from the other side, catching him on the left jaw.

"You little thief! What's that in your hand?"

Austin used a fist this time, a hollow thump on the left side of the ribs, followed quickly by a series of stinging slaps. Mike raised his arms to shield his face, and the matchbox fell out of his hand. He leaned over to pick it up, and another thump landed on his back. "Ow! I didn't take the matches, only the box!"

"They're *safety* matches, dumbass. They're useless without a box." Austin put out his hand. "Give it here."

There was a shuffling near the door. Bryan and Krisda entered the room, each going to his own bed. It was almost Lights Out, and there was nowhere else they could go.

Mike was shaking as he laid the matchbox in Austin's upturned palm. "Don't open it," he said.

"Why not?"

"Because." Mike looked at him pleadingly.

Austin snorted. He tested the little box's weight in his hand. Then he shook it, holding it close to his ear. A disappointed puff escaped his lips, and he shoved the matchbox drawer open with his finger.

Later, looking back, Mike would always blame himself for not speaking up. If only he had known Austin had a thing about spiders, he might have said something. But his mind was on so many other things, it didn't register until Austin started slapping himself, hopping around the room, twisting and jerking. "I'll *kill* you, you little punk!" Bryan and Krisda watched, open-mouthed, as Austin pivoted out the door and disappeared. They could hear him cussing all the way down the hall to the showers.

"Damn, what was that?" said Krisda.

"Oh no!" Mike dropped to the floor, searching on his hands and knees. "My spider!"

Bryan and Krisda looked at each other and laughed. But seconds later they were on the floor, too, helping him search. Krisda checked under the beds with his flashlight. Mike's voice cracked. "That bastard Austin. He killed my spider."

"Chill out, man," said Krisda. "If he was dead, we would've found his body by now."

"Yeah, he's probably hiding somewhere," said Bryan.

"I hope you find him, Mike. I wanna see that again."

His roommates fell into another giggling fit, but Mike was too upset to join in. He scoured every tile, every corner, and then started over again. Half an hour later, he was still on his hands and knees.

"Hey man," said Bryan, "we gotta turn the lights off, or—"

"Damn," said Krisda, "she's coming up the stairs!"

Mike, too, heard the heavy flick of sandals in the stairwell. The screen door creaking open and slapping closed. He jumped for the light switch. "Boys," Mrs. Watkins' voice echoed in the hall. "It's past time for Lights Out."

For a few seconds, nobody breathed. Mike stripped his clothes off in the dark, praying not to step on Peter by mistake. "Goodnight, Mrs. Watkins," Krisda and Bryan chorused innocently.

There was a long pause. Mike slipped stealthily into bed. Out in the hall, Mrs. Watkins' brain was ticking over, deciding whether they should be punished or not.

Then they heard the sigh and knew it was going to be alright. "Goodnight, boys," she said. The sandals flicked back down the hall. The screen door creaked open and slapped closed.

"*God*, Mike," said Bryan. "You and your damn spider!"

"Yeah, *Mike!*" said Krisda.

Chapter 21

The day the show went electric—bass thumping, drums popping—Shep's electric guitar took up a short, fast riff. On Mr. Stone's cue, Mike raised the microphone to his mouth to sing. After that, the world seemed to melt away.

Amplified, his voice sounded like it belonged to someone else. It wasn't just Mike singing anymore. It was Judas the man taking over Mike's body to tell about his pain. And his pain was *real*. He felt it as he watched from the fringes of the crowd—his best friend Jesus miming a sermon. The crowd lifting him on a bed of hands to carry him away.

When it was over, Mike came to himself kneeling on the stage, crumpled and spent. For a while his panting lungs made the only sound. Then his fellow cast members broke into applause.

"Beautiful," Mr. Stone gushed, clapping his hands. "What do you reckon, Mr. Jenkins, have we got a *hit* on our hands?"

"Absolutely gorgeous!" agreed Mr. Jenkins.

Then they made him do it again.

By the end of the third take, Mike was a wobbly mess. Mr. Stone took mercy on him and let him go home early. "Rest up, Judas. Save some of that adolescent angst for next time. We're doing the *Blood Money* scene tomorrow."

Mike tried to catch his friend's eye to say goodbye, but Jesus was already too far gone, kneeling in the Garden of Gethsemane.

Mike didn't have a ride home— "Mr. Ibrahim is not your personal chauffeur," Mrs. Watkins always reminded them—so he walked out of school to the bus stop on Holland Road. An old lady was sitting on the bench with her shopping in a canvas bag, watching the cars whizz by.

"*Salamat petang,*" Mike said in Malay. Then in Mandarin: "*Ni hao ma?*"

"Good afternoon," said the old lady. "You stay late after school?"

"Yes, auntie," said Mike, trying to be polite. He looked down the road through the tangled traffic but couldn't see any sign of a bus.

"Teacher punish you?"

"No. I'm in the play."

The old lady smiled. "Hollywood. Very good. Movie star."

They laughed together. Mike looked down the road again, but still the bus hadn't come. What he saw instead was a rickety sedan pulling up by the curb, coughing and sputtering through a leaky muffler.

"Mike!"

To hear his name shouted from a strange car was disorienting. To see Jin Kim leaning out the passenger window, even more so.

"Come, Mike! We fetch you home."

But Mike's feet had frozen to the ground, his stomach twisted in knots. *The Boy's Book of Spy Craft* should have prepared him for such a moment. Face-to-face with the enemy, behind enemy lines. The man at the steering wheel leaned across and smiled. "Eh, don't shy! Come let's go."

So that is what a communist looks like, thought Mike. Just like somebody's dad.

"Hurry lah!" said Jin Kim.

Mike waved apologetically to the old lady, who cheerfully shooed him away. He felt like he was in a body that didn't belong to him anymore, his arms and legs obeying alien signals from a distant spaceship. Here was his hand on the door handle, opening the door. Here were his legs climbing into the back seat. Jin Kim twisted around in his seat and grinned as the car sped into traffic. Mr. Chen's eyes studied Mike in the rearview mirror. "So how? Rehearsals going okay?"

Mike was about to reply when he noticed the briefcase on the seat next to him. It looked just like his own father's briefcase, except the leather latch-strap was a little more worn, and the color a more reddish shade of brown. This was the briefcase Mr. Keen had told him about. Mike's heart started doing somersaults.

"You okay?"

"Yes, sir," said Mike, coming back to his senses. "Sorry. I was just thinking about the play."

"Got two top stars in same car," said Mr. Chen, poking Jin Kim in the ribs. "And own son in title role. Didn't know I got such talent one!"

Jin Kim laughed. The next thing he said, Mike couldn't understand, because it came in a flood of Hokkien.

"Speak English," said Mr. Chen. "Where your manners, ah?"

"Mike got spider also, Pa," said Jin Kim. "Satu gonna fight him in World Championship."

Mr. Chen clicked his tongue. "Spider fighting not forbidden?"

"I *told* you, Pa, this school got no rules. Everything *bo cheng hu*."

"Oh, lai dat ah? Didn't they suspend you last time?"

Jin Kim scowled and looked out the window. Mike thought he saw the trace of a smile on Mr. Chen's face.

"So, Mike. Your parents in Vietnam?" Mr. Chen was looking at him in the mirror again.

Mike hesitated, wondering how much he could afford to give away. For an enemy agent, Mr. Chen seemed friendly enough, but of course that was part of the cover.

"Saigon, is it?" The man's eyes held him for a second more, probing. An impatience in his voice suggested more than just a casual interest.

"No, sir," said Mike, remembering to stay as close to the truth as he could. "They're still in Da Nang, I think."

"What they doing there?"

Mike affected a bored shrug. "They help people. Dad works for the U.S. Agency for International Development."

"Ah, okay." Mr. Chen braked for a traffic light. He put the gearshift in neutral and looked at Mike again. "Public Safety Division?"

Mike felt the blood drain from his face. Even Jin Kim looked up in surprise.

"*Pai seh*," said Mr. Chen. "Sorry, ah. Jin Kim told you I'm a journalist?"

Mike nodded.

"Neh mind, I just talk cock. Always after the big story." Mr. Chen chuckled as he stepped on the gas. The car gave a blast of acceleration, rounding the traffic circle onto Ferrer Road.

"You can just let me out here," said Mike. "I can walk the rest of the way. It's close."

"No, no," Mr. Chen insisted. "It's no trouble. This the turning here, is it?"

The old car coughed as it labored up the hill, shaded from the afternoon sun by a thick patchwork of leaves. It occurred to Mike for the first time that the enemy knew where he lived.

"Ah, very nice," said Mr. Chen as the car turned into the circular driveway. It was still free time, before dinner, and kids were playing or just hanging out in small clusters scattered over the grounds. Heads turned and looked as the car shuddered to a stop. Danny, playing with his toy trucks on the front steps, stood up and waved. "I was expecting *Oliver Twist*. But this very nice."

Mike's hand brushed the worn leather of the briefcase as he reached for the door handle. In a flash of insanity, he considered grabbing the bag and running for it. "Thanks for the ride, Mr. Chen," he said casually, stepping out of the car.

"No problem. S'okay."

Mike closed the car door and waved. But before he could take two steps, Mr. Chen called him back. "Eh Mike?" He leaned his head out of the driver's window. "Your parents. They ever talk to you about the Phoenix Program?"

Inside the car, Jin Kim was frowning at his dad. "Pa, let's go," he pleaded. But Mr. Chen ignored him, holding Mike a moment longer in his gaze.

"The *what* program?" said Mike.

Mr. Chen gave a small snort and waved his hand. "S'okay. Neh mind."

"See you, Mike," said Jin Kim.

"Bye."

This time Mike waited for the car to disappear around the bend before he turned away. His knees almost buckled as he headed for the dorm.

* * *

That night at Devotions, Mrs. Watkins talked about her hands. Sitting in the velvet armchair, the children gathered around her, she spread her fingers open in front of her and marveled. "Whenever I start to doubt, I look at my hands. Aren't they amazing? Alright, mine are old and veiny, but look at your *own* hands."

Some kids looked self-consciously at their hands. Some acted like goofballs, wriggling their fingers in parody.

"Think about it," she said. "These are God's hands."

Even the goofballs got serious now. Everybody was looking at their hands.

"What will God do with them?" said Mrs. Watkins. "They might be exactly the hands God needs."

A silence settled over them. A good, clean silence, full of the light in Mrs. Watkins' eyes. Mike felt love washing over him, scrubbing away all the dirty things he had ever thought or done. He caught Danny's eye, and Danny smiled back.

The clean feeling lasted all through the prayer, all through the song. But then it was over, and Shep put his guitar away, and the quiet multitude turned into a chaotic hive, kids jostling each other on their way back to the dorms. Mike stayed sitting on the floor with his back to the wall, partially hidden behind a potted plant. He watched as everyone left, doing his best to blend into the wall. He thought if he could make himself disappear, and just be here with God, he might hold onto the clean feeling a little while longer, though he knew it wouldn't last.

After everyone else had left, Mrs. Watkins called his name. "You can come out now, Mike."

Mike peered around the plant and saw her still sitting in the velvet armchair, her Bible in her lap. He scooted out from the wall and stood up. "Sorry. I must have fallen asleep."

But Mrs. Watkins wasn't fooled. "What is it, Mike?"

"Nothing." Mike didn't know what he wanted.

"I noticed you came home in a car." There was no scolding in her voice, because there didn't need to be. The facts were on her side.

"Oh, that," he said.

The lasers in Mrs. Watkins' eyes ignited briefly, then phased out. "You know the rules, Mike."

He nodded, and Mrs. Watkins' face softened a little. "Well, I suppose you have homework to do," she said.

"Okay." But still he didn't go. He brushed his hand along the piano keys absently, without playing a note.

Mrs. Watkins waited. She could wait for as long as it took. She had the kind of patience that could suck all the anxiousness out of a room and turn it into calm.

"What does *phoenix* mean?" asked Mike.

Mrs. Watkins blinked as if surprised by the question. "The phoenix is a bird from Greek mythology. It gets born again in fire and rises up out of the ashes."

"Born again?" said Mike. "That's like us. Christians, I mean."

"Yes, I suppose it is," she said, smiling at Mike. "It's wonderful how things are connected, isn't it? Rebirth is a theme in a lot of different cultures."

"But for us, with Jesus, it's real."

"Yes, that's right," said Mrs. Watkins. "It's certainly real for me."

"Me too," said Mike.

He felt the love coming off her like radiation. Which, after all, was what he had stayed behind for, what he had needed. But there was one other question he had to ask her.

"Mrs. Watkins, what's the Phoenix Program?"

She knitted her brow. "That I don't know, Mike. Where did you hear of it?"

Mike shrugged. "Nowhere. At school, I think. Goodnight, Mrs. Watkins."

"Goodnight, Mike."

He lingered in the warmth of her smile a moment longer before heading up to the dorm. He had work to do.

But back upstairs, his essay on *The Ugly American* stayed unwritten, his math problems stubbornly refused to be solved. He sat at his desk in front of an empty page, looking at his hands.

Chapter 22

Jason Keen was getting impatient. He sent his cheeseburger back to the kitchen, complaining that it was undercooked. His orangey cocktail was too warm, and he badgered the waiter for more ice. Now he was getting on Mike's case for not working fast enough. "We've got to get inside that briefcase," he said, tapping his knuckles on the poolside table.

Mike squirmed in his damp swimsuit. He had expected Mr. Keen to be happy, maybe even a little proud. He had just swum sixty-four laps of the Shangri-La pool without stopping. Not only that, but he was making real progress on the mission. He and Jin Kim were real friends now. He had even ridden in the enemy's car. But it seemed like nothing was ever good enough for Mr. Keen.

"We need to get Chen to give you another ride home."

Mike stopped nibbling on his club sandwich and looked up. Mr. Keen was doing his coin trick again, making a ten-cent piece crawl across his knuckles. But the fidgeting was more anxious than playful. He hadn't even touched his cheeseburger but was already on his third drink.

"You're going to have to take some initiative, Mike."

"What does *that* mean?"

Mr. Keen made the coin disappear from his hand. "What if you invited Jin Kim to spend the night at your place? If we play our cards right, Mr. Chen would drive you home after play practice."

"So?" said Mike. "I still couldn't get to the briefcase without him seeing."

Mr. Keen leaned in closer, pressing his elbows into the table. "You could introduce Chen to Mrs. Watkins, couldn't you? That would be the polite thing to do."

Mike shrugged. "Yeah, I guess."

"Suppose you forgot one of your schoolbooks in the back seat of the car. That would give you an excuse to go back."

Mike took another bite of his sandwich. "I don't know. Maybe."

"*Think*, Mike. You'd have maybe a minute, tops, to get his notebook out of the briefcase and take it to the dead drop. Could you pull it off?"

"But there'll be kids everywhere," said Mike. "Besides, it would be too weird."

"Why?"

"Nobody *ever* spends the night." Mike dropped his half-eaten sandwich onto the plate. He wasn't hungry anymore. Mr. Keen's bad mood was ruining his appetite. "Anyway, can't we slow down? Me and Jin Kim, we haven't been friends that long. And there's another thing…" Mike's voice trailed off.

"What?"

Mike dipped a French fry into a blob of ketchup and painted the rim of his plate. "Nothing," he said.

"Let's hear it," said Mr. Keen, his voice sharpening. "If you're having second thoughts about *serving your country*, let's have it out now!"

Mike dropped the fry and blurted, "I *like* him, okay? I didn't know it would feel like this." He pushed his chair back from the table and drew his feet up, hugging his knees.

When Mr. Keen spoke again, his voice was gentler, almost kind. "Of *course* you like him. He's your friend. But sometimes we have to make sacrifices, Mike."

Mike peered at him warily from behind a damp fringe of hair. "What about my parents?"

Mr. Keen didn't say anything. He gazed across the rooftop to the city beyond, as if the answer was somewhere out there in the haze.

Mike persisted. "You said. You *promised*. I did everything you told me to."

Mr. Keen put his sunglasses on.

"I know, Mike. I haven't forgotten. But we need you to do this thing for us, to carry it through. It could be the key to the communist movement in this part of Southeast Asia. We've both worked hard for this. Don't give up now. Okay?"

The waiter was approaching with the check on a small tray. Mike put his feet down and sat up.

"How many today?" asked the waiter.

"Sixty-four," said Mike. "A whole mile."

The waiter grinned. "Ice cream for champion one?"

"Not today," said Mr. Keen, signing the tab. "The boy is in training." He turned his mirrored lenses on Mike as if to preempt any protest. There was nothing more to say.

Chapter 23

Mike cinched his sarong and scuttled out of the room and down the hall. Already the showers were steamy and on full blast, the bathroom crowded with half-asleep high school boys. Austin was at the sink now, bearded with shaving cream, scowling at Mike from the mirror. Mike scampered into a stall to pee.

"Heard about your run-in with that spider," Shep's voice burbled from under the shower.

Laughter.

"You gotta admit it was funny, Austin."

More laughter.

Austin's voice now: "That little jerk is gonna *die*."

Nobody was laughing now. There was no sound at all except the spray of the showers.

Mike left the toilet unflushed, slipping out of the stall as quietly as he could, praying for God to make him invisible. *Thou art my hiding place; thou shalt preserve me from trouble; thou shalt compass me about with songs of deliverance.*

At breakfast he was careful not to give away any more than he had to. The success or failure of the mission could hinge on Mrs. Watkins' answer to the question he needed to ask. Mike almost hoped she would say no.

He bided his time, stirring his corn flakes, waiting for a lull in the animated buzz of conversation. Danny had her ear, as he usually did this time of day, entertaining her with his third-grade adventures. Mrs. Watkins had gone a little glassy-eyed, and Danny's mouth was full of cereal. Mike took the chance to make his first move. "Is it okay if I have a friend over to spend the night?"

Mrs. Watkins took a sip of her coffee and winced. "Well, it's a little unusual. Who might this friend be?"

"Just a friend from school."

He would tailor his lies to be as vague as possible. *The Boy's Book of Spy Craft* said it was important to maintain plausible deniability in case anything went wrong.

Mrs. Watkins frowned. "You're a little old for sleepovers, aren't you?"

Mike fought back the urge to argue. He was always either too old for something, or not old enough. But now wasn't the time to press that point. The moment required a more delicate maneuver.

"We need to practice our parts. We're both in the play. Plus, we can help each other with our Mandarin homework."

"Does he play ping-pong?" asked Danny. "We can have a tournament!"

Mike dropped his spoon, splashing droplets of milk on the table. Danny had just wrecked his opening gambit. "Sure, we can play, but only after we finish our homework. We'll have *lots* of homework, though."

"Cool," said Danny.

Mrs. Watkins' face was an enigma. The cogs in her brain were turning, but Mike couldn't tell in which direction.

Danny giggled. "I heard about the spider."

Mike kicked Danny's foot under the table.

"What spider?" said Mrs. Watkins, frowning.

Mike smeared the spilled milk with his thumb, at the same time nailing Danny with his fiercest gangster stare.

"Nothing," said Danny. "I was just kidding."

"I hope you boys aren't pestering spiders. Some of them might be poisonous."

Check. In her distracted state, Mrs. Watkins hadn't exactly given him permission, but she hadn't *not* given permission, either. Mike started gathering his dirty dishes to make his getaway.

"Mike, I'd really feel better if I could talk to the boy's parents."

Mike froze. "I don't think they have a telephone," he said, and immediately regretted it—she would see through that lame excuse for sure. Still, she hadn't exactly said no yet. Mike had to execute his next move carefully.

"Maybe he could bring a note," he suggested helpfully. "From his mom, I mean."

Mrs. Watkins sighed. Her resolve was weakening. "You'll be responsible for your guest. Making sure he's comfortable, keeping him entertained."

Danny said, "I know! We can take him to see that new horror movie. *The Exorcist.*"

Mrs. Watkins sputtered into her coffee, looking bug-eyed as she half gagged. Mike took his chance. This time she didn't stop him as he bussed his dishes to the kitchen hatch and made his escape.

Check mate.

It wasn't until several days later that Mike broached the subject with Jin Kim. Between play rehearsals and preparations for the spider fight, there hadn't been enough time to bring up the question. At least, that's what Mike told himself.

"Mighty Peter versus Satu Number One, World Spider Fighting Championship. Admission price five dollar. What you think, Mike?"

They were working on the posters. Mike hadn't had the heart to tell Jin Kim his spider had gone Missing In Action. He still held out hope that Peter would resurface in time.

"We should add *lightweight*," said Mike. "It sounds more official."

"Satu not lightweight!" said Jin Kim. "Satu heavyweight, like Muhammad Ali."

"But he's skinny."

The librarian hissed at them from the check-out desk. They ducked their heads down, pretending to busy themselves tidying up the mess of cardboard and magic markers strewn across the table.

"Not *skinny*," Jin Kim whispered indignantly. "Satu very fit, lah."

They finally agreed on "welterweight," and added an illustration: two hairy spiders with savage cartoon faces, one biting the other's leg off. They worked without speaking, and in the contented silence, Mike found his courage. "What are you doing this weekend?" he asked. "It's

Shep's birthday on Friday, there's going to be a party. You want to come spend the night?"

Jin Kim looked up from the poster he was coloring. "Eh? Spend what?"

"Sleep over," said Mike. "With me."

Jin Kim scrunched up his face. "What talking you? I catch no ball."

"*You* know," said Mike. "Stay the night at my house. At the hostel, I mean."

Jin Kim's jaw dropped. "Sleep whole night? At the orphanage?"

"It's not an orphanage!"

The librarian shushed them again, glaring over the tops her glasses. "It's not an orphanage," Mike repeated quietly. He bent his head down until a fringe of hair shrouded his eyes. "Anyway, you don't *have* to come. Just forget it." The tip of his magic marker squeaked against the cardboard.

Jin Kim sighed. "This spend night thing, I never did before. See first, lah."

Mike looked up, incredulous. "You never spent the night away from home?"

Jin Kim shook his head. "What ghosts you got? Happy ones?"

"Ghosts?" Mike snorted.

Jin Kim looked at Mike with pity in his eyes. "*Ang moh*, you so blur like sotong! Ghosts *everywhere*, man. Got be nice to them, give them nice things."

"Oh, *that*." Mike thought of the little red shrine set up outside the staff quarters. "The amahs take care of that. Rice cakes and incense."

Jin Kim looked dubious. "Hungry Ghost month coming. Need more than just rice cake."

"Okay, *whatever*. Bring some fruit or something. They like fruit, don't they?" Mike was shocked to hear such words coming out of his own mouth. But if the mission required humoring pagan spirits, that's what he would have to do.

Jin Kim's face brightened. "Pomelo and mango. *Shiok*, man! Make happy ghosts."

Chapter 24

The briefcase sat next to him in the back seat, guarding its secrets. The windows were open to an inrush of mild evening air. Still Mike sweated, his school shirt pasted to his skin. In front, Jin Kim and the communist prattled back and forth like characters in a TV show. They spoke in English, but Mike wasn't following what they said. He was too busy panicking about tonight's covert operation. All the tactical scenarios Mr. Keen had gone over seemed suddenly harebrained. It wasn't going to work. He would have less than a minute to get into the briefcase, extract the notebook, and take it to the dead drop. It was asking too much.

Not only that, but there would be kids everywhere. Scattered in small groups across the lawn, on the basketball court, at the outdoor table, playing or talking or horsing around. Just like any Friday afternoon when school was a whole weekend away.

The car labored around the bend at the top of the hill, and the hostel came into view. Mike quietly slid his schoolbooks off his lap and laid them on the floor between his feet.

"Okay," said Mr. Chen, pulling to a stop in the circular driveway. He set the emergency brake and looked at his son. "Joy yourself."

Jin Kim's body stiffened. "You going now?"

"I not invited to sleepover," said the communist. He touched Jin Kim under the chin. "Don't worry. Morning come fast."

Already the plan was unraveling. Mr. Chen was supposed to get out of the car, but instead he just sat there. "Wait!" Mike said, digging his fingers into the plastic upholstery. "Mrs. Watkins wants to meet you."

The communist looked at his watch. "She want talk to *me?*"

"Yes, sir. To get your permission."

Mr. Chen sighed. It seemed to take him forever to move. Finally he reached for the door handle. "Okay, let's go." From the basketball court, Shirts and Skins ogled them as they got out of the car. Then Austin slapped the ball out of Shep's hand, and the game started up again.

"Pa, the fruit!" said Jin Kim.

"*Pai seh*. Almost forgot." Mr. Chen fished out his keys again and opened the trunk. "Mother pack for you some clothes also."

Jin Kim used both hands to juggle the fruit basket and a paper bag half filled with clothes. Mike closed the back-seat door gently, trying to act casual, hoping they wouldn't notice that his hands were empty. "This way, Mr. Chen," he said.

Mrs. Watkins was at her usual place this hour, in the nook that served as her office, writing a letter at her desk. You always knew she would be there, like a piece of old furniture. She turned in her chair as they came in. Her face looked old, until her smile brightened it, like the sun coming up in the morning, like you always knew it would.

"Well, who have we here?" Mrs. Watkins stood up, laying her fountain pen aside, and offered Jin Kim her hand. "Welcome, Jin Kim. Mike's told us so much about you."

"All lies," said Jim Kim as he shook her hand.

Mr. Chen frowned.

A flicker of confusion crossed Mrs. Watkins' face. Then she laughed, before offering her hand to the communist. "And you must be Mr. Chen."

"Sorry ah," he said, looking askance at his son. "Nice to meet you."

"I'm glad we got a chance to meet," she said, "since you don't have a telephone."

"Eh?" Mr. Chen wrinkled his brow. "Got telephone."

"Oh, but I thought—" Mrs. Watkins looked at Mike.

"Oh, dang!" said Mike, slapping himself in the head. "I left my books in the car. Be right back!" He took off running before anyone could stop him. He flew past the mail table and leapt down the front steps into the driveway, his feet plowing gravel as he reached the car.

He took a quick look around, then yanked the car door open and ducked inside. Sweat poured off his face in the oven-like heat. The leather of the briefcase felt soft, almost human, when he touched it. He fumbled with the latch. His hands were shaking horribly. The jaws of the briefcase snapped open, and he peered inside.

In a brown paper bag he found the remains of Mr. Chen's lunch. Half a chicken sandwich and a cluster of rambutans. Suddenly he wanted to cry. He thought: *I'm stealing from my best friend's dad.* But that couldn't be true. A covert operation wasn't the same as stealing. It was just the *feelings* again, sneaking around inside his brain. It was no good trying to ignore them, he thought. You had to crush the feelings. You had to smoosh them and crumple them like a paper ball and fling them in the trash.

He rummaged some more until he found the notebook—it had a spiral binding and pages filled with hastily scribbled notes. He hid it carefully between his math textbook and his daily planner. Then he closed the briefcase and snapped the latch into place. The plastic-upholstered seat burned his knees as he backed out of the car.

"What are you doing, Mike?" a voice said.

Mike wheeled around, knocking his elbow against the car door. The books spilled from his hands, strewing across the gravel at Danny's feet.

"Uh oh," said Danny, squatting down to help.

"Don't touch that!" Mike snatched the notebook out of Danny's hand.

"Jeez, sorry." Danny's face started to crumple.

"No, it's okay," said Mike. "I didn't mean it. I'm just a little nervous."

"Because your friend is spending the night?"

"Yeah, I guess."

He waited for Danny to run off and play, but the third-grader stayed where he was, looking puzzled. Mike glanced toward the basketball court and the patch of jungle beyond. There was no way he could make it to the dead drop in time, not with Danny sticking to him like glue. He would have to improvise.

"Sorry, Danny, I gotta go. They're waiting for me."

"Are we gonna play ping-pong later?"

"Sure thing!" He tucked the books under his arm and ran for the TV room.

Luckily, it wasn't a big TV night, just a few kids watching the tail end of *Gunsmoke*. Nobody paid attention to Mike hovering around the bookcase. Nobody saw him slide the notebook between volumes 18 and 19 of the *Encyclopedia Britannica*.

When Mike got back to the assembly room, Mrs. Watkins was giving Mr. Chen a tour of the photographs on the wall above her desk—old grainy black-and-whites of her missionary days. Here was Mrs. Watkins smiling outside a kampong. Mrs. Watkins riding a water buffalo through a rice paddy. Mrs. Watkins looking gaunt after being released from a Japanese prison camp. Mrs. Watkins cutting a cake on her wedding day.

Jin Kim balanced on one foot, then the other, clutching his basket of fruit. Even Mr. Chen was starting to look a little glassy-eyed. "Mike, why don't you show Jin Kim to your room?" said Mrs. Watkins.

Mr. Chen touched his son on the shoulder. "Okay lah, see you."

Jin Kim's eyes went fawn-like. "You going now?"

"In a minute. After I talk with the auntie."

"Okay." Jin Kim swallowed, his face already slack with homesickness. "Bye."

Mike felt sorry for him. His stomach filled with butterflies, in sympathy, as he led the way upstairs. It really did feel like an orphanage sometimes. Like when they first went away, leaving you here. The next time you saw them, they were strangers.

"It's only for one night," said Mike.

The amahs had set up an extra cot next to Mike's bed. Jin Kim perched on the edge, holding the fruit basket in his lap, staring across the room. A great emptiness was opening up inside him, Mike knew, and something had to be done before it swallowed him whole.

Mike sat down next to him and hung an arm around his shoulder. The bony warmth of Jin Kim's body, the closeness, made his eyes water. His voice sounded choky when he said, "Let's get changed. You wanna play ping-pong?"

Jin Kim was mute as he stood up and began unbuttoning his school shirt. Mike went over to the dresser and fished out a pair of shorts and a T-shirt. He wished Jin Kim would say something. The sounds coming in from outside—the playground shouts, the bounce of the basketball, the far-off rush of traffic on Ferrer Road—deepened the silence between them. But then they heard the car sputtering in the driveway, churning gravel under its wheels as it passed.

Jin Kim, hearing the sound of his father leaving, seemed to acknowledge that some new phase had begun. The tension in his face loosened. "No," he said at last, picking up the fruit basket. "First we feed the ghosts."

Chapter 25

The ghosts would have to wait. Getchu was already making her rounds, ringing her heavy handbell. "Dinner ready! Time for *makan!*" The bell clanged inside and outside, in the dormitories, in the TV room, on the lawn, on the basketball court. "Time for *makan!*"

The basketball game was declared a draw. Skins put on their shirts. The TV switched off. Bare feet thumped down dormitory stairs. Children gathered before the table of a great feast. The coolest among them feigned boredom, but most didn't even try. The excited hum was palpable. *Tacos. Tacos. Tacos!*

"We'll do it later," Mike said, watching the blur of teenage boys past their door. "It's tacos tonight. For Shep's birthday."

"Don't play play," said Jin Kim seriously. "Ghosts hungry, lah. Been waiting longtime."

"After dinner," Mike said.

But Jin Kim couldn't be persuaded to leave the fruit basket behind. He hugged it to himself as they joined the barefoot parade down the stairs. The screen door slapped and banged, boys filled in the ranks behind them, there was no way out but down. A tall kid tapped the dangling lightbulb just to show off, and their shadows flew about the stairwell like hysterical specters. Somebody whooped. In disorderly cadence, their feet slapping tile, a marauding tribe.

Tacos. Tacos. Tacos!

In the dining room, Shep was already looking embarrassed. The girls were making jokes about his dimples. He smiled at the floor as the hubbub of voices reached full pitch. The Happy Birthday song wouldn't be till later, but in the meantime he had to endure the ribbing.

Jin Kim observed the goings-on with a studied interest. His grip on the fruit basket relaxed a little. When a peal of laughter rang out, he stood on tip-toe to look.

Mike watched Jin Kim, wanting him to like it here. *See?* he wanted to say. *We have fun. We're not orphans!* But a hush was already descending on the crowd. Mrs. Watkins stood patiently in front of them, laser-beaming the remaining holdouts with her stare, until everybody got quiet and bowed their heads. All except for Jin Kim. Mike peeped an eye open, and they exchanged a conspiratorial smile. For a moment it felt like they were on the same side. But what side was *that?* Everything was getting confused.

Tonight Mrs. Watkins took longer to say grace, throwing in some extra thanks for birthday boys and special guests, but finally she reached the Amen. Shep and Jin Kim were herded to the front, and a pair of lines formed behind them. Mike fought his way past Ming to get a place in line behind Jin Kim. He figured his guest might need help with the fixings, since he'd never seen a taco before.

"Mrs. Watkins, Mike's cutting in line again!"

"No, I'm not. I'm helping."

Ming made a face, and Mike grinned back at her smugly.

"You put the meat in first, like this," he explained to Jin Kim, showing him how. "Then some lettuce on top of that. Then some salsa on top of that. Then…"

Jin Kim was a fast learner, and cool under pressure, and a minute later they were carrying their plates to one of the big tables. Except Jin Kim had to make an extra trip back to retrieve his fruit basket.

"What's with the fruit?" Bryan asked.

Jin Kim shrugged. He set the fruit basket on the table and studied his tacos warily.

"Yeah man, we got cake and ice cream tonight," said Krisda. "You don't gotta bring your own dessert."

"Not for me," said Jin Kim. "For the ghosts."

Bryan sputtered, a taco halfway into his mouth. "Ghosts? What ghosts?"

Krisda slapped Bryan's arm, causing his taco to explode. "You *idiot.* Hungry Ghost Festival. Don't you know anything?"

106

"Oh *that*," said Bryan, trying to rescue the debris from his taco. "I thought that was a Buddhist thing."

Krisda kicked him under the table. "*God*, Bryan."

Bryan winced. "What?"

"Maybe he *is* a Buddhist, you idiot."

"Oh." Bryan looked at Jin Kim with his mouth open, the remains of the demolished taco still in his hand.

Jin Kim scowled. "What? Never see before?"

Mike tried to change the subject. "You have to hold your head sideways," he said to Jin Kim, demonstrating the correct method of taco-eating. "Like this."

"But what's he gonna do when *they* get here?" said Bryan.

They. Mike knew who he meant. Any minute now, the hostel would be overrun by Bible-toting teenagers.

"Yeah, *Mike*," said Krisda accusingly. "You can't take him to *Bible* study."

"I'm not!"

Jin Kim screwed up his face. "Bible what?"

Bryan glared at Mike. "You didn't even tell him?"

"Uncool," said Krisda, shaking his head. "That's so *Ugly American*, man."

"Shut up," said Mike. "We're not *going* to Bible study. I already have a plan for that."

But just what the plan was, Mike didn't know. He had been so focused on tonight's covert operation, he hadn't thought that far ahead.

"Don't worry, Jim," said Bryan, slapping Jin Kim on the back. "We'll take care of you."

And that was how it started. Step by step, in almost invisible maneuvers, Bryan and Krisda began stealing his friend. And Jin Kim was almost complicit in the crime. He seemed to enjoy the attention, and didn't even complain when they called him "Jim." He laughed at their jokes. He listened when they explained the hostel's quaint traditions.

"After the cake, we ambush him outside," Bryan said.

"Ambush?"

"It's his birthday," Krisda explained. "Seventeen licks."

"Oh, no, not *that* again," said Mike. He felt a need to a draw a line somewhere, but was helpless to explain why.

"*God*, Mike. Take a chill pill. It's only for fun."

After that, things just got worse. Someone turned off the lights, and a procession of amahs carried in a cake with seventeen candles burning. Shep was red-faced, but there was nowhere to run. He had to endure the birthday song, followed by extra choruses of "You Live in a Zoo." Conspiratorial glances were cast over cake and ice cream. Shep must have sensed the danger, knowing he would have to make his escape soon if he wanted to keep the element of surprise on his side. But Mrs. Watkins hadn't yet left the table. Her presence seemed to hold a protective spell over everyone. But, like most magic, it was only an illusion.

Mrs. Watkins stood up. "My, that was delicious," she said, balancing cup and saucer in hand. She turned toward the kitchen, as she always did, to give Getchu her compliments. Everybody watched. Every eye followed her until she disappeared through the door.

Then, as if a switch had been flipped, every head in the room turned to Shep. His last spoonful of cake stopped mid-way to his mouth. His eyes darted left and right under a fringe of hair. The spoon fell from his hand as he leapt up from his chair, his lithe body twisting in air toward the open French doors behind him. Simultaneously the deranged tribe rose in gleeful pursuit.

"Get him!" shrieked Ming.

Chair legs raked the floor. War whoops flew. Bodies blurred past in open stampede. Only Mike was left sitting at the table, staring at a pool of melted ice cream on his plate.

Mike helped Getchu clear the tables, then headed for the bookcase and pulled out a volume of the *Encyclopedia Britannica*. Getchu eyed him curiously over a stack of dirty plates. "Mike, you okay? Why not play with other children?"

Mike shrugged. "I don't like that game." He flipped through the encyclopedia pages, then slid volume 18 back into place. When he left through the open French doors, he was clutching a reporter's notebook in his hand.

He disappeared into the jungle patch, blending into the shadows, and returned a minute later empty-handed. The notebook was safely lodged in the fork of a stunted tree behind the basketball court. Exactly where Mr. Keen would know where to find it.

Kids were already arriving for Bible study by the time Mike got back from the dead drop. A taxi chugged into the driveway, its headlights briefly illuminating a small riot on the lawn. Shep was being dragged out of the tree where he had sought refuge. Ming, grinning, tested the ping-pong paddle against her palm. The mob howled.

"What's going on over there?" asked Patrick, jumping out of the taxicab.

Mike sighed. "Shep's birthday."

"Oh, that. Ha-ha." Patrick pronounced the laugh like a word from the dictionary, but his expression was eager, like always. "If we hurry, we can bags the sofa. Go get your Bible, and I'll save us a spot."

"Oh. I'm not coming to Bible study."

Patrick frowned. "What do you *mean* you're not coming to Bible study?"

"I mean, I can't come," Mike said. "I have a guest."

"So? Bring him with."

"He's not a—" Mike paused, trying to think of the right way to say it, but there was no right way. "He's a Buddhist or something."

"Oh *God*."

Mike was surprised to hear his friend use the Lord's name in vain. "It's only for tonight," he said.

Patrick narrowed his eyes. "It's that Chinese kid, isn't it?"

"Jin Kim. I think he's Singaporean, actually."

"What*ever*," said Patrick. "People have been *talking*, you know."

Mike couldn't think of any good reason why the hairs on the back of his neck were standing up. Even so, his voice trembled a little when he said, "About what?"

"You and him. It isn't right that he's playing Jesus."

Mike screwed up his face. "What are you *talking* about?"

Patrick looked at Mike with hurt in his eyes. He turned on his heels to march away, but halted abruptly. The specter of Jin Kim, carrying a basket of fruit, had materialized out of the darkness. Patrick drew in a sharp breath and stared.

"Time to feed the ghosts," said Jin Kim. "Where got altar?"

Oh, good grief, thought Mike. Patrick clutched his Bible tighter, giving Jin Kim a wide berth as he edged toward the assembly room. In just a few a minutes it would be front-page news. The night was quickly turning into a disaster.

Jin Kim sighed impatiently. "No time. Where got altar? Nighttime already, lah."

"The amahs keep one in the back. I'll show you." Mike cast a pleading look at Patrick. "We're going to play Risk after. Why don't you come? It'll be fun."

Patrick's eyes widened, then narrowed again, like he had seen the Devil. He shook his head slowly and said, "I'll pray for you."

Mike felt the hurt rising in his throat as he hurled the insult back. "I'll pray for you, too!"

The red dollhouse-like box stood on a table next to the wall, its interior carefully decorated with paper ornaments, faded photographs, and small dishes of food. Tendrils of sweet smoke rose from the tips of joss sticks. Mike had always known the altar was there, but seeing it up close shocked him.

Jin Kim seemed to approve. But he wouldn't touch the altar himself. "Where the aunties?" he said.

"What aunties?" said Mike.

Jim Kim rolled his eyes. "*Ang moh,* don't be kayu. The *aunties,* man! Who take care of the ghosts?"

"Oh, that." Mike looked around uncertainly at the concrete walkway, the red-brick walls. He had never been this far back into the staff quarters. Though he thought he recognized some underwear hanging on the clothesline that might be his own. "We're really not allowed back here," he whispered.

Jin Kim shrugged. "Neh mind. Only take a minute." He went up to a door and made a fist to knock.

"No, wait!" said Mike. "You can't just—"

But he did. He just knocked.

The door was opened by a small woman, hardly bigger than Mike. A toddler was playing on the concrete floor behind her. She said something to the child in Teochew, which even Jin Kim didn't understand. To the boys she spoke only in smiles, accepting the fruit basket graciously.

"You see?" said Jin Kim as they made their way back. "Ghosts happy now."

Chapter 26

With the added cot, the small room was already a sea of mattresses. It didn't take much to push all four beds together to form a giant trampoline. Krisda somersaulted from one springy mattress to the next as The Rolling Stones blasted from the stereo.

"Turn it down!" said Mike.

"What?" said Bryan.

"Turn it down! You're going to get us in trouble."

"What?"

Bryan cupped a hand to his ear and shrugged. He mouthed the words *"I can't hear you"* and jumped onto the giant trampoline, which had now become a kind of stage. Krisda and Bryan strutted from bed to bed in their socked feet, singing "Sympathy for the Devil" into make-believe microphones. But even that wasn't the worst thing. Now Jin Kim jumped onstage to join them.

Mike, an audience of one, huddled against the wall. Wishing he had never invited Jin Kim to spend the night. Wishing he had never met Jason Keen.

"You're disturbing the Bible study!" said Mike.

"Oh my God!" Bryan slapped himself in mock horror. "We're *disturbing* the Bible study!"

Krisda mimed being struck by lightning and fell down dead, his limp body jouncing on the mattress.

Jin Kim laughed. Mike glared at him with dagger-eyes, but Jin Kim didn't see him at all.

"Poor Mikey," said Bryan. Then his eyes lit up. *"I know!"*

"Yeah, man!" said Krisda, bouncing back from the dead. "Only one thing can cheer Mikey up."

Bryan: "This is a job for…"

Bryan and Krisda in unison: "Charlie the Tiger!"

A full-scale alarm went off in Mike's head. He scampered across the mattresses on his hands and knees, but Krisda got to the dresser first, digging into Mike's drawer in a frenzied search.

"I'll kill you!" screamed Mike. Running out of mattress like a jet crash-landing at the end of a runway, he tumbled to the floor.

Krisda held the tiger above his head, victorious. "Charlieeee!"

Mike leapt up from the floor and grabbed, but his hand swiped empty air. Charlie dangled just out of reach. Krisda, giggling, tossed him over Mike's head. Mike pivoted, leaping onto Bryan's bed, but Charlie was already airborne again, sailing in a high arc, narrowly missing the blades of the ceiling fan. This time it was Jin Kim who made the catch. "Wah, tiger is it?"

Mike turned a deeper shade of red. "Give it here," he said, breathless, reaching out a hand. "It's just a stupid toy I had when I was a kid."

Jin Kim looked at Mike and grinned.

Mike made a grab, but missed. Jin Kim faked a pass to Bryan, then tossed the tiger high toward Krisda instead. Charlie went sailing again, higher and higher into the stratosphere, into the blurry, whirling blades of death.

Whock! Velvet fur met the sharp edge of steel. Two blurry projectiles spat out from the ceiling fan, slamming into walls on opposite sides of the room.

The Rolling Stones still blasted away, but nobody was singing along anymore.

"Oh, no!" said Bryan, laughing. He leapt to his stereo and hit the kill switch.

The speakers went dead. Out of the sudden silence, a Bible study song drifted faintly on the warm evening breeze. *This little light of mine, I'm gonna let it shine…* The ceiling fan whirred.

Mike knelt at the decapitated body of Charlie the Tiger. The others might have mistaken his frown for bereavement—but no, it wasn't really that. There was something odd about the headless stuffed toy in his hand. Something sticking out of the stump of the neck that didn't quite belong.

Jin Kim put a hand on his shoulder. "Sorry, Mike."

Underneath the song, Mike heard the whisper of Mrs. Watkins' sandals on the stairs. The screen door creaking open and closed. Now the flick flick flick of footsteps in the hall.

"Let it shine, all the time, let it shine…"

Now Jin Kim was frowning too. "What is it?" he said, staring at the object in Mike's hand.

But Mike didn't have time to answer. The door was already opening. He thrust the thing into his pocket and kicked Charlie under the bed. He would give him a decent burial later.

It wouldn't have been a real sleepover without getting in trouble at least once. Mrs. Watkins had to ascend the stairs twice more before they were finally quiet. The ghost stories kept them awake longer—not stories at all, really, but a catalog of facts, rumors, and half-baked memories, which Jin Kim told in matter-of-fact detail, as if he was giving an oral report at school. "Must be careful also of the *pontianaks*," he said.

"The what?" Bryan's voice wavered on the other side of the dark.

"*Pontianaks*," said Jin Kim. He lay on his back with his hands behind his head, looking up at the ceiling. His eyes glistened softly as he spoke. "Grandmother told me."

Krisda laughed (a little nervously, Mike thought).

"What, you don't believe?" said Jin Kim.

Bryan snorted. "Go ahead. Tell us."

Jin Kim seemed to shrug in the dark. "They hang upside down in the trees, waiting for children to pass."

"Wait," said Krisda, uncertainty creeping into his voice, "why are they hanging in trees?"

"They hungry," said Jin Kim softly. "So they hang in the tree in the park, waiting longtime for the children. Got long bloody tongues. So when the children pass, the *pontianaks*—" Jin Kim made a wet slurping sound with his tongue. "They suck the blood lai dat."

It wasn't as if Jin Kim was trying to scare anyone. He was only

114

imparting factual information to some clueless American boys who might need to know. At some point they fell quiet, and the night swelled with jungle sounds—the sawing of insects, the warbling of anonymous birds, the sighing of trees. A gecko, caught in a shaft of moonlight, scurried across the wall.

In the morning, Jin Kim's eyes were crusty with sleep dust, his hair messed into a mop. "I know what it is," he croaked. "I see before."

Mike pulled the sheet down from his face and squinted, half-asleep. "Huh, what?"

Jin Kim sat up in his cot, blinking at the sunlight. "That thing in the tiger."

They scampered down the hall to the bathroom, their bare feet slapping the tiled floor. Jin Kim got to the urinal first, so Mike took the stall. They sighed in exaggerated relief.

"Are you going to tell me or not?" said Mike. "What *is* that thing?"

"Microfilm," said Jin Kim.

"Micro-*what?*"

"Need machine to read, lah. I see before where my father works."

Mike hadn't yet comprehended, and as he struggled for under-standing, his aim faltered, and he almost missed the toilet bowl. "So what's it doing in my tiger?" he said.

All through breakfast the question nibbled at his brain. How long had Charlie been hiding his secret, and why? It was the kind of puzzle he would normally have taken to Mr. Keen, but their next Martial Arts lesson was still days away. Besides, it felt too personal—like a message from his mom across the borderlands of childhood—a secret message for Mike alone.

Jin Kim also knew the secret, but he hadn't told. Even as he shone in his new-kid glow, the center of attention at the breakfast table, he remained steadfast. Even when Bryan made him tell again about the *pontianaks*—a story less scary in daylight, but weird enough to make Mrs. Watkins almost choke on her hardboiled egg—he did not waver or fall.

Chapter 27

Across the reference desk, the librarian narrowed her eyes. "What would *you* need a microfilm reader for?"

Jin Kim blinked as if he hadn't understood the question. "For reading microfilm," he said.

Mike cringed. He had warned Jin Kim about the librarian, but Jin Kim hadn't listened. His so-called coolness under pressure was going to get them in trouble.

Mrs. Range's eyes flashed like a werewolf's. "Well, bless your *hearts*," she said, standing up behind her desk. Her hands settled on the hips of her frumpy dress. "And I guess you want some microfilm to go with that?"

Mike's fingers closed around the bulky reel in his pocket. Jin Kim started to say something, but his voice trailed off. He glanced sideways at Mike.

There was no time for thinking at all. "Operation Phoenix," he blurted. The words came out of the deep and dark, like Excalibur rising from the magic lake. "We're researching Operation Phoenix."

Whatever it might have meant, the phrase worked like a magic spell. The librarian deflated as some of the hot air leaked out of her. "You're not old enough for that," she said. "Heck, *I'm* not old enough. Was it that radical Mr. Stone put you up to this?"

She didn't wait for an answer. She disappeared behind a row of high dusty shelves. "You coming or not?"

Mike hesitated. "Back there?"

Back there was where the banned books were kept, where the secret rites of bookbinding and other librarian dark arts were performed. It was alien territory.

116

The librarian was all business. "Sit," she said, pointing to a desk pushed against the wall. On top of the desk was a dusty machine, and two chairs had been set up in front of it. The librarian left and came back a minute later with a small cardboard box which she set on the desk in front of them.

Mike read the label. *The New York Times, Jan-June, 1970.* He didn't dare touch the box.

Mrs. Range pointed out the controls. "That button turns it on. The reel goes here, thread the film through there, stick the end of it here. This button is forward, that one is back. The date you want is February 18th."

Mrs. Range folded her arms and watched as they threaded the film into the machine. "It ain't exactly rocket science," she said. Then she left them there.

Mike looked around. Shelves were cluttered with old books, odd-looking stationery, index cards, rubber stamps. A million dust particles floated in a ray of sunlight. "Do you think they keep the sex books back here?"

"Maybe," said Jin Kim. Everybody knew about the sex books, but nobody had ever seen one. "Anyhow, no time for that. Lunch almost over." He pressed the fast-forward button on the machine, and a blur of black-and-white newsprint raced across the screen. It took them several stops and starts to get to February.

"Too many ads," said Jin Kim, pressing the button again. Page after page whizzed past.

"Wait! Stop!" Mike pointed at the screen. "Go back."

Jin Kim tapped the rewind button. "*Wah liao!* Look, Mike." In the picture, a young man was being thrown off an armored personnel carrier, hands tied behind his back. Jin Kim read the caption: "The Controversial Operation Phoenix: How it Roots Out Suspects."

Mike's jaw dropped. There was something wrong with the picture. Or maybe they had got the words in the caption mixed up. "This isn't right," he said. "We're the good guys."

Jin Kim looked at him. There was almost a tenderness in his voice when he said, "*Ang moh*, why you so blur, man?"

117

"I'm *not* blur," said Mike. "This has to be a mistake."

A silence grew between them. Mike's breath came out shaky. He searched the article again for some proof he could show Jin Kim.

But Jim Kim was already pushing back his chair. "Lunch time over," he said. "Let's go, Mike."

"But we haven't even looked at Charlie's reel yet."

"Class started already."

"I'm staying. You go." He felt a lump in his throat when he said it. He didn't want to be left alone with the reel in his pocket.

"Teacher make trouble for us," said Jin Kim.

"You go," said Mike.

"*Big* trouble. Send to office, call home."

"So? You don't have to stay."

Jin Kim looked at him. His eyes were dark and deep. The knot in Mike's throat grew tighter.

Finally, Jin Kim threw up his hands. "Okay. Hurry lah!"

They had to work fast before the librarian came back. Jin Kim pressed the rewind button, and the pages whizzed backwards in a blur.

"Come on, come on!" Mike looked over his shoulder. The librarian hadn't yet appeared in the space between the high shelves.

The screen flashed white, and the tail end of the film whipped round and round. Jin Kim's fingers fumbled taking the reel off.

"Hurry up!" Mike held Charlie's reel ready in his hands. He snapped it into place on the spindle. His hands shook as he threaded the film through the machine.

Jin Kim's finger was poised over the button. "Ready?"

Mike nodded. But he was not ready at all for what he saw.

Chapter 28

They came for Jin Kim in the middle of Mandarin class. The school secretary was unsmiling when she said his name from the back of the class-pod.

"Jin Kim, bring your things."

"Eh?"

If they told you to bring your things, it meant you weren't coming back. Everybody watched Jin Kim gather his notebook and textbook and pencils. They were glad he was the one in trouble and not them. Mike waited for the secretary to call his name too, but she didn't. Jin Kim looked at Mike one last time before he turned to go. *They found out*, his eyes said.

Mrs. Lee tried to catch everybody's attention again. But Mike was still turned around in his chair watching Jin Kim go. He looked small as he followed a step behind the secretary, head bowed. He pushed through the glass doors, and in a flash of sunlight, he was gone.

"你要去哪里?" said Mrs. Lee.

"我要去学校了," said the class.

Mike blamed himself. He should have known the librarian was a double agent. It had to be her who had ratted them out.

"Mike, pay attention," said Mrs. Lee.

They would want to know who else was involved, to add to their list of names. They would get a full confession from Jin Kim before they came for Mike.

"你念哪所学校?" said Mrs. Lee. She was looking right at him.

"What?" said Mike.

Mrs. Lee put her hands on her hips. "Mike, can listen or not?"

"Can," said Mike.

119

"你念哪所学校?" said Mrs. Lee again.

Stacy Wong helpfully raised her hand. "新加坡美国学校," she said.

"Very good, Stacy," said Mrs. Lee.

Mike slid lower in his seat until his chin was level with the desk. He closed his fingers around the spool of microfilm in his pocket, feeling its shape. If they caught him with it, he was in deep trouble. But he couldn't let Jin Kim face the firing squad alone.

Mike raised his hand. "Can I use the bathroom?"

Mrs. Lee made him say it in Mandarin before she let him go.

When Mike got to the office, Jin Kim was nowhere to be seen. Only the usual suspects were lined up on the Time-Out bench. The sixth-grade delinquents eyed him suspiciously as he walked in.

Mike went straight to the reception desk. "I'm here to confess," he told the school secretary. "I did it."

"Eh? Did what?"

"I mean it was *me*, not Jin Kim. I'm the one who should be in trouble." Mike looked at the closed door of the principal's office, imagining a broken Jim Kim on the other side, slumped in a wooden chair.

The secretary's frown softened. "Jin Kim not in trouble. He have to go home early because of family emergency."

"Emergency?"

"That Mr. Chen very brave one," she said, shaking her head. "Wrote another story government not like. Police came to house, arrested him."

Mike gaped at her. "Did they say why?"

"*Mm chai si*, that one. Not scared of nothing."

"What was the story?"

The secretary shooed him away. "Say too much already. Go back to class now."

After school, Mr. Ibrahim barely had time to set the emergency brake before Mike threw open the van's sliding door and leapt out. He raced for the TV room, dumped his schoolbooks on a chair, and turned on the English-language news.

"*Straits Times* journalist Simon Chen has been detained under the purview of the Internal Security Act," the newsman announced through the static fuzz of the TV screen.

"Why are we watching this?" said Ming. "When's *Star Trek?*"

Mike listened with growing alarm. Something had gone terribly wrong. They were supposed to be helping people, not hurting them. He didn't even *care* anymore if Mr. Chen was a communist, not after what he'd seen on the microfilm.

All through Study Hour, his pen hovered uselessly over a blank page. No matter how hard he tried, he couldn't unsee what he had seen. The images flashed through his mind in grainy black and white.

"Jesus, Mike!" Bryan hissed from his desk. "Cut it out!"

Mike hadn't noticed his leg going berserk under his desk, pumping up and down like a piston.

"Some of us are trying to study. If you don't *mind*."

"Yeah, *Mike*," said Krisda.

Mike held his renegade knee down, staring at his blank paper, trying to remember the protocol for an Emergency Rendezvous. Somehow, he had to reach Mr. Keen. He had to talk to him tonight.

"Only in an absolute emergency," Mr. Keen had said when he gave Mike the business card. *"Press the buzzer three times, and then return to the rendezvous point. Wait for me. I'll find you."*

Mike could feel his roommates' eyes on him as he crossed the room to the dresser. Normally he would have been more circumspect, but tonight there wasn't time. He dug up the argyle socks his mother had bought for him two Christmases ago, the ones that were too dorky to wear, which stayed balled up in a far corner of his drawer. Tucked inside he found the business card and slipped it into his pants pocket. "I'm going to the bathroom," he announced.

Bryan looked at him deadpan. "Gee, thanks for telling us, Mike. Like I really needed to know that."

"Number one or number two?" said Krisda.

"Don't forget to flush."

"Go chase yourself," said Mike.

It was hard to act normal when you were on a mission. You had to keep your cool and stay focused, even if your heart was burning to spill the beans. Mike wished more than ever he could tell Bryan and Krisda who he really was.

Down the hall he found the door to Austin and Bill's room slightly ajar. He raised a fist to knock, but then thought better of it—it was still Study Hour. He poked his head through the opening instead.

Bill, studying at his desk, saw Mike first. He opened his mouth to speak, but then he hesitated. His eyes darted sideways at Austin, who was lounging on his bed in a sarong, reading *Moby Dick*.

Austin's instincts were immediately aroused. He put his book down. In another second he crossed the room, grabbed the front of Mike's shirt and twisted it into a noose. "It's Study Hour, dumbass," he said, hauling Mike into the room. "You want to get us all busted?"

"I know, I'm sorry," said Mike, letting his body go loose like a string puppet. "But I need to talk to you." He glanced at Bill, who was staring hard at his chemistry textbook, pretending to study. "I need to talk to you alone."

Austin snorted. He let go of Mike's shirt and pushed him into the hall. "In my office," he said, giving Mike another shove.

Mike stumbled forward, regaining his balance just in time to be shoved again. Three more shoves and they were in the bathroom. Austin dragged him into a shower stall and pressed him against the wall. "You got my attention," he said.

Mike's breath came out ragged. The older boy's arms formed a cage around him. He could feel Austin's muscled body radiating heat, the details of his tough-guy smile blurring into a collage of eyes and lips. "I need your help," said Mike. "I need to break out of the hostel tonight."

Austin's smile faltered. His eyes narrowed. Mike knew the rage was coming next and he had to get his words out fast.

"I know you guys do it all the time. You have a secret passage. You sneak out on Saturday nights to go to Boogie Street."

Austin's hand slapped the wall next to Mike's head. "It's *Bugis* Street, you idiot. And what makes you think—"

"You *have* to help me," said Mike. "Or I'll tell Mrs. Watkins what you did at the American Club. How you sold me to that guy."

"What the—"

Hearing the confusion in Austin's voice, Mike pressed in for the kill. "Mr. Keen gave you money, didn't he?"

Austin let go of the wall and took a small step back. Incredulity and anger wrestled on his face. "This is bullshit," he said. "I didn't *sell* you. He just wanted to meet you."

"It's okay," said Mike. "I promise I won't tell, ever."

Austin studied Mike hard, an unfamiliar look creeping into his eyes. "You little scumbag," he said. But there was a tinge of respect in his voice. "What the hell are you up to?"

"None of your business," said Mike. "Oh, and I'll need some money, too."

Chapter 29

The taxi driver squinted at the address on the card, holding it up to the light. Then he looked dubiously at Mike. "This place no good," he said. "Not for children, lah."

"But I'm thirteen," Mike said. "I pay adult price at the movies."

The taxi driver clicked his tongue. "Bad place. Very dangerous for *ang moh*. Come let's go, I fetch you home."

"But I don't want to go home. Look, I'll pay extra." Mike opened his fist to show the small wad of bills he had extorted from Austin. "How much?"

A small gleam appeared in the taxi driver's eyes. Competing scruples wrestled on his face. He looked at Mike. "Twenty dollar."

"No way!" said Mike. "I pay you ten. There and back."

"For you only, my friend. Fifteen dollar. Very special price."

Mike sighed, pretending to be annoyed. "You rob me."

"Very good price. Come let's go."

Mike climbed into the back seat, which smelled of stale cigarettes and puke. The driver glanced at him in the rearview mirror as they pulled away from the curb.

"Your parents not worried?"

Mike shrugged, resting his forehead on the window, watching the city lights flash by. It was such a pain having to explain things to people over and over. "My parents aren't here."

The driver looked ahead at the road, but the frown stayed on his face. "Who take care of you?"

Mike wanted to tell him to mind his own business. "I live at a hostel," he explained.

"Orphanage, is it?"

"I'm not an orphan!" said Mike. "I just *live* there."

"Okay. Sorry ah."

Traffic was light. The taxi drove through parts of town Mike couldn't remember seeing before. Everything looked different at night. Sleepy neighborhoods gave way to busy nighttime markets where couples wandered among gas-lit stalls. Vendors fried spring rolls and noodles in vast steaming woks, their faces flickering in the gas flames. Skimpily dressed women paced the sidewalk, or stood alone in shadowy doorways.

"You want I wait for you?" said the taxi driver, pulling over into a side alley.

Mike looked out the window. "This is the place?" A single bulb above a doorway illuminated the alley. Young men in flared jeans sat on their parked motor scooters, smoking cigarettes. They turned their heads to look at Mike as he got out of the car.

"I wait for you," said the taxi driver. "Five minutes."

Mike checked the number on the card as he walked past the motor-scooter gang, feeling their eyes shift as he passed. A woman in a miniskirt stepped out of the doorway. Her face was painted-on, and her fingernails looked fake. Mike knew he had seen her before. "Wah, very *jude* one," said the Lady of the Night, reaching out a hand to touch his hair.

Mike flinched. The motor-scooter boys laughed.

"Eh don't shy. See no touch, is it? *Sayang* ah! You want come home with me, I fix you nice dinner. What money you got?"

Was this really the same Lady of the Night who had sat next to Jason Keen in church, who had kissed him at the American Club pool? There was something in her eyes that did not seem real. Something in her voice that was as fake as her nails.

"No thank you," said Mike. "I'm here to see someone. Is this number 31?"

"Staff entrance only," said the Lady. "Anyhow, not for children. Go home now."

Mike hesitated. Mr. Keen's instructions had been clear. *"Press the buzzer three times, then return to the rendezvous point."* The button for the buzzer was right there on the wall, but this woman stood in his way. She pointed a finger into the night and said, "Go home."

Mike had no choice but to turn away. The motor-scooter boys traded smiles. One made a joke in Hokkien, and the others laughed.

Mike didn't take it personally. *The Boy's Book of Spy Craft* said it was normal for agents in the field to encounter unexpected obstacles. When that happened, sticking to protocol wasn't always the best answer. Sometimes you had to get a little creative.

Staff entrance only, the Lady of the Night had said. That meant there must be another door somewhere. Mike just had to find it. He broke into a run, sprinting past the taxi to the end of the alley, rounding the corner at full speed.

His sneakers skidded on the pavement. His body slammed into a colossus-sized wall of flesh. A smiling giant in sunglasses grabbed him by the ear and pulled his face up to the light.

"*Kiam pah* ah!" said the bouncer. "Why so havoc, boy? This not a playground."

Mike dangled from the giant's ferocious pinch. He peaked sideways to read a flashing neon sign: Lion City Lounge.

"Sorry," said Mike, wincing. The whole universe was suddenly concentrated in his screaming earlobe. He pushed himself higher on the tips of his toes. "I need to see Jason Keen!"

The giant tweaked his ear again, and Mike gasped.

"Mistah Keen very busy. What for you want?"

"I have a message for him. Look, he gave me his card." Careful to hold his head just right, he fished the business card out of his pants pocket.

The bouncer let go. Mike crumpled, pressing a hand against his throbbing ear.

"*Mm chai si*, is it?" The bouncer held the card up to the light. "Not scared to die?"

Mike blinked against the mist in his eyes. "Mr. Keen will want to see me. I'm a friend of his."

"Mistah Keen got many friends. Enemies also got. How I know you not bad one, ah?"

Mike opened his mouth to reply, but hesitated. He didn't know what the right answer was. "You're a bad one, too," he said finally.

The bouncer grinned. His monster-sized hand encircled the back of Mike's neck and steered him toward the entryway. "Come," he said. "Not keep Mistah Keen waiting."

The glass door opened into a pandemonium of sin. Half-naked ladies danced on a narrow strip of stage as a Rolling Stones song blasted from the walls. Waitresses in skimpy skirts carried trays of cocktails across the smoke-filled den, delivering them to crowds of drooly-eyed men transfixed in the hypnotic blink of strobe lights. Mike tried to avert his eyes as he stumbled forward into the abyss.

The bouncer never let go. He kept his grip even when Mike stumbled, holding him up by the back of his shirt collar. In this way they zigzagged between crowded tables toward the bar, where a thin, cold-eyed man in a bowtie was drying cocktail glasses with a dirty towel.

"What you want I do with this bad one?" said the bouncer. "He looking for Jason."

The bartender studied Mike with his cold eyes. Then he looked at the bouncer, gesturing toward a dark corridor with a cock of his head. "You know what." He set one glass down and picked up another.

The bouncer nodded and shoved Mike past the bar into the darkness beyond. For a second his feet left the ground, his shirt half strangling him, buttons popping loose under his chin. His feet found stairs, and he climbed, stumbling.

Now I lay me down to sleep. In his terror, it was the only prayer he remembered.

They passed an altar with smoldering incense. Slits of light under bedroom doors. A child crying somewhere. In another room a couple were arguing in Cantonese. Music from downstairs reverberated off the walls, the bass pulsing through the floor.

I pray the Lord my soul to keep.

At the end of the hall, they came to a door.

"No, please," said Mike, when he saw what was planned for him.

"You wait here," said the bouncer, pushing him inside. The door closed in Mike's face. A key turned in the lock.

Mike barely had enough room to turn around. Sweat prickled his face as he felt around in the inky darkness. His hands found the wet head of a mop, but no light switch. His shoulder raked a shelf, sending cans and boxes and utensils crashing to the floor. Acrid fumes of disinfectant stung his eyes and throat. He held his breath, listening to the bouncer's footsteps receding down the stairs. *And if I die before I wake...*

Mike crumpled to the floor and sat, hugging his knees. His body tingled with the dread of punishment. All his lies and manipulations, all the bad things he had done. *I pray the Lord my soul to take.*

Chapter 30

Mike was barely half-awake when the angel came for him. With all the holy light shining behind the angel's head, Mike mistook him for Jesus.

"Are you taking me to Heaven?"

Then he knew it couldn't be Jesus, because the angel said: "Not yet, kid. Not yet." Mike tried to stand up, but it was too hard. He staggered in a half crouch, as if his body was loaded down with iron weights. Angel feathers brushed against his face. Then he felt the strong arms lifting him, cradling him, his head lolling against a warm shoulder. Mike stopped trying to open his eyes then and just let himself be carried. He didn't know where the angel was taking him, but it didn't really matter. Wherever it was, God would be there.

When he opened his eyes next, he felt a mattress under him. A shadow moved against a plastered wall.

"You've gone too far this time, Jason," said a woman—a voice that sounded familiar, but somehow changed. Mike saw her in a corner of the bare room, sitting on a wooden chair. The miniskirt, the makeup, the fake-looking nails. "You never should have given him this address."

"Do you think I *intended* for this to happen?"

The room was lit by a bare bulb hanging from the ceiling. The harsh light chiseled away at the boyish contours of Jason Keen's face, making him look older than he was.

"It was only to be used in an emergency," Mr. Keen said. "He broke with protocol. He disobeyed my instructions."

The Lady of the Night put a finger to her lips, sitting up in her chair. She had caught Mike watching them. "He awake now," she said.

Jason Keen turned his head. In an instant he was kneeling at the bedside, his hand on Mike's forehead, brushing back the sweaty hair.

"I'm sorry," Mike croaked. His throat felt dry and rough, like it had been sandpapered.

Mr. Keen shushed him. "Don't worry about that now."

The Lady of the Night stood at the door, pouting her red lips. "Accuse me, boys. I go now." She looked at Jason Keen and shook her head.

"Wait a second," said Mr. Keen. He went out into the hall with her and closed the door. Mike could hear their muffled voices arguing on the other side, but he couldn't make out what they said. A minute later Mr. Keen came back in with a glass of water.

Mike's hand shook as he drained the glass. Water had never tasted so good.

"You want to tell me what this is about?" said Mr. Keen. The mattress sagged as he sat on the edge of the bed. He took the glass from Mike's hand and set it on the desk. "You want to explain to me what is so damned important that you risked both our lives? Not to mention the mission—what were you *thinking?*"

"It's our fault," said Mike. "Mr. Chen's in jail because of us."

The furrows on Mr. Keen's forehead deepened. "Mike, listen to me. That had nothing to do with—"

"Liar!" Mike swung his feet to the floor and stood up too fast. Dizzying darkness shrouded his eyes. He staggered, waiting for his vision to clear. Mr. Keen's hand touched his shoulder, and he shied away. "It's all a bunch of lies! We're not even the good guys!"

Mr. Keen sat upright on the edge of the bed, staring at him with a hurt look. "What do you mean?" he said. "Of *course* we're the good guys."

"No, we're not!" Mike paced back and forth, hands fisted at his sides, breathing hard through his nose. "I need to pee," he said finally.

"Listen, Mike—"

He jerked open the door and went out into the hall. He found the door marked 'WC' and went inside. The toilet was a ceramic slab cemented on the floor with a hole in it. His aim was shaky, and he missed a lot.

When Mike got back to the room, Mr. Keen was sitting in the

wooden chair. A spiral-bound notebook lay on the desk next to him. "You might as well see for yourself," he said.

Mike glanced warily at Mr. Keen as he stepped up to the desk. The notebook was familiar to him—the same one he had lifted out of Mr. Chen's briefcase and then hidden in the fork of a tree—but still, his hands trembled when he picked it up. He flicked through page after page scribbled in shorthand English and Chinese. The shocking humanness of the scrawl filled him with shame. "He's not a communist at all, is he?"

Mr. Keen turned his hands palms up. "There wasn't much action-able intelligence, if that's what you mean."

"Then why—"

"I take orders, same as you, Mike. They don't always tell me what I'm looking for. Or why."

"We have to help him."

"I'll see what I can do." Mr. Keen put out his hand. "You better leave that with me."

Mike clutched the notebook at his side. "I'm taking it back to him."

"You can't," said Mr. Keen, weighting his words with patience. "People will ask questions. Surely you see that."

"I don't care," said Mike. He opened the door to the hall. He paused and looked back as rock music swelled from downstairs. "I have to. It's *his*."

Mr. Keen stood up, his frown darkening. "Mike, for Chrissake!"

In the second before Mr. Keen lunged, Mike took off running. A wild guess told him the stairs were to the right, and he took them one landing at a time, bouncing off walls with the notebook clutched in his hand. He tripped on the last stair and fell sprawling into the smoke-filled nightclub, staggering to his feet just in time to run face first into a waitress. She slapped him.

Face stinging, he weaved between crowded tables, ricocheted off drunks, skidded between dancing couples under the flashing strobe. The bouncer stepped in front of the door, grinning like a defensive tackle across the line of scrimmage. Mike dived head first, sliding across the waxed floor. The giant's hands grappled at his wriggling body but couldn't get a hold. Mike slithered out the door into the fetid night air, stumbling again to his feet, cutting a sharp left toward the alley. *Please, God.*

The taxi was still there. Mike yanked open the back door and dived inside. "Let's go!"

The taxi driver woke with a start. "Eh?"

"Get us out of here!" shrieked Mike. He pulled the door shut and locked it.

The taxi driver glanced in the side mirror and straightened up, suddenly alert. The engine coughed, sputtered, then roared, as footsteps pounded the pavement behind them.

"Go!" Mike slammed the driver's seat with his fist.

The car lurched backwards, tires squealing. A man-shadow leapt out of the way, then ran alongside them into the street, pounding on the window. "Mike, don't do this! You're putting yourself in danger!"

The taxi screeched to a stop, narrowly missing a satay stall, then lurched forward into the crowded street, horn blaring. Pedestrians scattered. Mike knelt backwards on the seat, watching the running figure through the rear window. Mr. Keen didn't slow, even for a second, arms pumping in a flat-out sprint, shrinking to almost nothing before he faded into the night.

Chapter 31

Sneaking into the hostel wasn't as hard as sneaking out. Mike curled up on the leafy path behind the basketball court, using the notebook as a pillow, until he heard the roosters crowing. By then the amahs were already up and about doing their morning chores, and Mr. Ibrahim was rolling up his prayer mat. Nobody paid any attention to Mike.

Climbing the dormitory stairs, the tiredness caught up with him. He stashed the notebook under his mattress and crawled between the sheets without even taking off his clothes. It seemed only seconds later that Bryan was leaning over him and shaking his shoulder. "Jeez, Mike, get up already! We're gonna be late."

Mike pulled Charlie out from under his pillow and held him close. Not because he needed the company, especially, but because he needed to make sure the tiger's head was still attached. It had taken him forever to sew it back on. The stitching was clumsy, but the microfilm was safely inside. Satisfied, Mike pulled the sheet up over his head and closed his eyes.

"*God*, Mike!"

"I don't feel good," he said.

There was a pause. "You want me tell Mrs. Watkins you're sick?"

Mike pulled the sheet back from his face and studied his roommate. Bryan would really do that for him, and Krisda would back him up, too. They would even add little eyewitness details—coughs in the night, feverish dreams—to make the story more convincing.

But playing sick with Mrs. Watkins was serious business. There would be thermometers involved, and a lot of questions. In his present sleep-deprived state, he could easily slip up. Besides, there was something important he had to do.

"What's that, your secret diary?" said Bryan as they climbed into the Volkswagen bus.

Krisda laughed.

Mike scrunched himself into a far back corner of the van, clutching the notebook tighter to his chest. He tried to think of a witty comeback, but he was too tired.

"Shut up," he said.

Mike had never skipped school before; never even thought himself capable of it. But there were a lot of things he had never done before, until now. Lying with impunity, going AWOL at night, stealing—his sins were too many to name. But it seemed that God in his silence was asking him for one sin more.

Escaping from school was surprisingly easy—he simply walked off the grounds unnoticed. Two bus rides later, he was outside the Straits Times headquarters on Kim Seng Road, a fortress-like building with a concrete tower. Some kids on a school field trip were lining up at the front entrance. Nobody said anything when Mike attached himself to the back of the line. Nobody seemed to care that he was *ang moh*, or that his pants were a darker shade of blue.

The lady leading the tour smiled a lot. She walked backwards while talking, pointing out the sights as they went. Everybody was in a hurry to get to the exciting stuff—the monster printing presses with their giant rolls of newsprint. Nobody cared about the newsroom with its labyrinth of cubicles, reporters sweating into white collared shirts, tapping out their stories one alphabet letter at a time. Mike waited as the line of kids snaked away. He checked twice to make sure they were gone, then ducked his head into the nearest cubicle.

"Excuse me," he said. "Do you know Simon Chen?"

The reporter stared back through tendrils of smoke, a cigarette dangling from his mouth. "Maybe," he said. "Depend who ask."

"I have something of his," said Mike, showing him the notebook. "Can you give it to Mr. Chen when you see him? When he gets out of jail, I mean."

Peering through smoke, the reporter regarded Mike with a one-eyed squint. "Give it your ownself can." He reached backwards and knocked on the partition wall behind his head. "Eh, Jun Ling, some *ang moh* big shot to see you."

There were some rustling sounds in the neighboring cubicle, and a man's head popped up above the partition. "Mike! What you doing here?" Mr. Chen's face showed surprise, then puzzlement. He saw the notebook and frowned.

"I got your notebook," said Mike.

Mr. Chen's eyebrows danced above the partition wall. He gestured at Mike with his hand. "Come inside. Nosey reporter got some questions for you."

Mr. Chen's cubicle was even more cramped than the other guy's. A clunky typewriter sat in a swamp of papers and news clippings and tattered files. The partition walls served as a makeshift bulletin board plastered with photos, maps, handwritten notes, scraps of documents with scribbles in the margins. Mr. Chen lifted a stack of files off the spare chair and dumped it on the floor. "Sit. Don't shy." He plunked himself into the worn-out swivel chair behind the desk. "So, you got my notebook. Where find?"

"I didn't *find* it, exactly," said Mike. "I more like, stole it."

They looked at each other across the typewriter. Mr. Chen toyed with a pencil, tapping the eraser end on the desk. "Okay. Want give it back or not?"

Mike handed the notebook over shakily. "Sorry," he said. "I thought you were a communist."

Mr. Chen opened the notebook and flicked through the pages. "You only steal from communists?"

"I'm the reason you got arrested," said Mike. "It was my fault."

"Big police informant is it?" Mr. Chen chuckled. "Neh mind. Police don't need a reason to arrest me, Mike. They only want to intimidate. The government is very sensitive, they don't like bad press."

Mike gripped the sides of his chair. "I'm not in trouble?"

"Eh?" Mr. Chen dropped the notebook on the desk and looked at him across the swamp of papers. "I not your father, Mike. But I worry about you, okay? Someone put you up to this, or what?"

"I can't tell you. It's classified."

Mr. Chen stared for a minute with his mouth open. The sound of clacking typewriters swelled around them. Mike felt comforted by the racket, as if the noise could drown out his fears.

"Someone is using you, Mike." Mr. Chen leaned forward, resting his elbows on a pile of news clippings. "Don't you think?"

Mike studied the reporter cautiously. "Why did you ask me about Operation Phoenix? Even Mrs. Watkins never heard of it. Why did you ask *me?*"

"You know what is Operation Phoenix?"

"Yes. Maybe. I don't know. Something about… pacification?"

Mr. Chen snorted. "Nice euphemism. It's a killing program, Mike. Set up by the CIA to target Vietnamese civilians suspected of communist sympathies. Except they use nice big words to describe it. *Pacification*, hah! But that's old news now."

"If it's old news, why did you ask me about it?"

"Smart one." Mr. Chen tapped a finger against his temple. "What's my angle ah?"

"Are you going to tell me or not?"

Mr. Chen grinned. "I tell you one word, okay? *Drugs.*"

He chuckled like a schoolboy as he stood up and leaned across the desk, pointing to a map on the partition panel next to Mike. It had different-colored thumbtacks pinned into it, with strings of yarn radiating out to photos in the margins. "You see here? This a map of the main heroin smuggling routes through South East Asia. This one from Laos to Saigon by air. This one overland from Burma to Bangkok. This Phoenix Program very expensive deal, right? Lots of bribes to pay. Killing cost money. So where the money come from, you think?"

"The drugs?"

"Steady lah! Smart boy."

Mike traced his finger along a string of yarn. "Who's this?"

"Those guys the big shots in South Vietnam. That one General Quang, he runs the operation so President Thieu can keep his hands clean. These Navy guys also very important. See here? Some of the heroin and opium travels from Saigon by ship."

136

"Where does it go?"

"That the big question!" Mr. Chen tapped his finger on a thumb-tack in the Saigon River. "Until now, the heroin went to Hong Kong. From there, Chinese syndicates moved it to Europe and United States. But now I think the strategy is changing. This guy Mr. Big in Thailand, he fighting with the Hong Kong bad guys now. So maybe Hong Kong not so safe anymore."

"You think the drugs are coming through Singapore?"

Mr. Chen shrugged. "Maybe." He harvested a thumb tack from the edge of the map and planted it at the southern tip of the Malay Peninsula. "Singapore. Got big international harbor. Central location in South China Sea. Why not?"

"I don't get it," said Mike. "What does this have to do with me?"

"You tell me, Mike." Mr. Chen sat down again and leaned back in his chair. "Got something for me or not?"

Mike felt the reporter's eyes on him, probing and questioning, but also seeming to offer something. A recognition, perhaps. And with that recognition, a way out. He wasn't a secret agent, not really. He was a kid. He had carried the secret so long, it seemed only fair that he should be allowed to give some of it away. Give it to an adult to handle.

But Mike had a promise to keep, and faith the size of a mustard seed to make it true. "I'm supposed to be at school," he said.

Mr. Chen offered his hand, and they shook. "S'okay, Mike. But if you change mind…" He tucked a business card into Mike's shirt pocket. "Call me anytime."

Chapter 32

When they send a lieutenant colonel, you know it can't be good news. But Mike was already having the worst day of his life even before he saw the Army uniform.

At school he'd got sent to the office for being AWOL and had to spend his whole morning break on the Time-Out bench. Then, all through lunch, Jin Kim kept asking about Peter, the spider who was still Missing In Action. Mike tried to hedge, but in the end he had to stoop to another lie. A few times he'd almost choked on his *nasi goreng*.

Even now, as the old Volkswagen bus labored up the steep jungle road toward home, the fried rice sat like a brick in his stomach. Wriggling shoulders jostled him on either side, and for a second, he thought he might spew. Bryan and Krisda started singing "With a Little Help From My Friends" really loud, and Krisda punched Mike in the arm because he wouldn't join in. A fight broke out, and Mr. Ibrahim had to stop the van. It was torture waiting in the suffocating heat for the van to start up again, while the driver glared at them in the rearview mirror.

"Please, Mr. Ibrahim, let's go!"

But Mr. Ibrahim could hold out longer than anybody. "No fighting," he said, mopping his forehead with the white handkerchief he always kept neatly folded in his shirt pocket.

"Yeah, *Mike*," said Krisda accusingly.

Mike started to protest. "I wasn't—"

"Jesus, *Mike*," said Bryan, thumping him on the back. "Stop horsing around!"

"You're in *so* much trouble," said Krisda.

Mr. Ibrahim's eyes darted back and forth in the mirror, not sure who to settle on. He put the van in gear, and everybody sighed, and nobody said a word, as a cooling breeze chased the hot air out again. At last they came to a stop in the circular driveway, and kids started spilling out, a blur of blue and white uniforms. But Mike couldn't move. His hands had turned into claws, gripping the back of the seat in front of him.

"Mike, let's go!"

"Hurry up!"

"Any day now, Mike!"

Even Mr. Ibrahim turned around in the driver's seat to look at him. "Boy. You okay?"

Then the others saw it, too—Mrs. Watkins by the front door, talking to the Army guy—and everybody fell quiet.

Mike jumped out and made a beeline for the dorm, schoolbooks flapping at his side. He felt the heat of Mrs. Watkins' laser-beam eyes. The war ribbons on the officer's chest screamed in technicolor as he hurried past.

"Just a minute, Mike."

He stopped. His stack of schoolbooks came apart and tumbled onto the driveway. He squatted to pick them up, fingers scraping gravel. Blood deserted his brain as he stood up again. He anchored his eyes on the war ribbons until the dizziness went away.

"Sorry," said Mike. He didn't know yet what he was in trouble for, or how much they even knew, or what the colonel's visit meant. But he had a pretty good idea.

"Mike, you remember Colonel West, from the Embassy?"

Mike nodded. The colonel was here to tell him that his parents were dead. He had got dressed up in his war ribbons to do it. He had polished his shoes.

"Come inside and let's talk."

Mrs. Watkins led the way, and the colonel planted his hand between Mike's shoulder blades to steer him along. In the assembly room Mrs. Watkins perched on the piano bench, and the colonel took the velvet armchair. Mike dumped himself into a sofa on the other side of the room, scrunching himself small against the armrest.

"I'm afraid I have some bad news," said the colonel.

Mike felt a sudden pressure behind his eyes. He had to hold his face together, or it would break into pieces.

"It's about your martial arts instructor, Mr. Keen."

"Huh?"

Mrs. Watkins' eyes shifted from the colonel to Mike. "This is not your fault, Mike," she said. "It's important that you know that."

"Mr. Keen may not be what he seems," said the colonel. "We have reason to believe he might be—" The colonel paused, hunting for the right word—"*dangerous.*"

Mike swallowed. "Dangerous?"

"He's a contractor who did some work for us a while back, but we had to let him go. Since then, he seems to have gone rogue. We think it's possible that he's working for the other side." The colonel leaned forward in his chair. "I'm sorry to have to ask you this, Mike. But Mr. Keen seems to have taken a special interest in you. Any idea why that might be?"

"No, sir," said Mike. "I mean, I can't think of any reason."

Mrs. Watkins and the colonel looked at each other. They both seemed relieved.

"Mike, if Mr. Keen tries to contact you again, it's important that you let us know right away. We've already alerted the school and the police."

"The police?"

"Jason Keen is a fugitive now," said the colonel. "He's desperate, and there's no telling what he might do. You understand?"

"Yes, sir," said Mike.

"And there's one other thing." The colonel shifted in his chair. "This is a little delicate. It can't leave this room..."

Mrs. Watkins looked at Mike. Her eyes had gone all soft.

"We're still trying to figure out how *you* fit into this." The colonel looked embarrassed and coughed into his hand. "Mike, is there anything you haven't told us? If you're in possession of any material that your parents might have passed onto you for safekeeping... Well, that's something we need to know about."

"Material?"

"Information," said the colonel, leveling his eyes at Mike. "Information of a *sensitive* nature. Documents or photos or other materials that could be dangerous if they fell into the wrong hands."

"You mean like... *secret* stuff?"

The colonel nodded. "Yes, Mike. Secret stuff. If you *were* in possession of classified material, that would be a federal crime. Do you understand?"

Mike stared. He couldn't find his voice.

"It's important that you think about this carefully."

The colonel was looking at him as if he were some kind of criminal. Mike pulled his feet up and pressed his back deeper into the sofa, digging his hands into the spaces between the cushions.

"Colonel," Mrs. Watkins said, frowning. "I think that's enough."

"I don't *have* any secret stuff," said Mike.

Mrs. Watkins had already stood up. Her voice was polite but firm. "Thank you, colonel. I'm sure we'll be in touch if Mike remembers anything more."

The colonel eyed her sheepishly like a schoolboy caught shooting spitballs. "Yes, of course," he said, standing up.

Mike didn't wait to be excused. He grabbed his schoolbooks and raced upstairs.

"Hey, Mike. Everything okay?"

Bryan and Krisda had already changed clothes, and the stereo was pumping full blast.

Mike yanked open his dresser drawer and plunged his hands in.

"Mike, what's wrong?"

Socks and T-shirts and underwear flew from the drawer and piled at his feet. "Where *is* he?"

He skidded across the room and checked under his pillow. He dropped onto his hands and knees and searched under the bed. He crumpled on the floor with his head in his hands as his roommates stared.

"He's gone," said Mike. "Charlie's gone!"

Chapter 33

It wasn't Mike's problem anymore, Miss Kumar assured him. "There are people who care about you, who are going to keep you safe," she said. Under interrogation, Mike had been forced to give up some details about his meetings with Mr. Keen. But he hadn't told her anything of value. He hadn't betrayed their secret—the only secret that really mattered.

Miss Kumar seemed to know he was holding back. "I wouldn't be surprised if you had some ambivalent feelings about Mr. Keen. He was your friend, after all."

Feelings. Mike kept his mouth closed and tried not to show any emotion at all. He would crush the feelings, squeeze them into pulp, throw them to the ground and squish them under his Bata sneakers.

"My point is, Mike, it's okay to feel a bit confused. It's only natural." Miss Kumar tilted her head sideways and smiled girlishly. "Now tell me all about this *Superstar* play. Dress rehearsal today, is it? How exciting!"

It was a relief to throw himself into the play and think of nothing else. He and Jin Kim had been working on their scenes together every free minute they could steal. It was only an act, but that made it all the more real. Judas felt what Mike couldn't dare to feel. "Can we try the arrest scene again?" he asked on their way to get changed.

"No time, lah," said Jin Kim. "Need get makeup already."

One of the learning pods in Beta Community had been turned into a makeshift dressing room for the boy actors. They took off their uniforms and stuffed them into paper bags labelled with their names. Scruffy tunics made of old rice sacks went over their heads, cinched at the waist with a rough length of rope. For a minute they stood looking at each other.

"I feel like a dork," said Mike.

Jin Kim clicked his tongue. "Not got beards yet," he said hopefully. "Need beards."

In the pod next door, Mrs. Range and a team of parent volunteers had set up makeup stations. Mike flinched when Mrs. Range came at him with an eyebrow pencil. "Can we just skip to the beard?"

"Hold still," she said. Mike's squirming only made her more determined.

"I'm the bad guy," said Mike. "You're supposed to make me look tough."

"That's a tall order," said Mrs. Range.

"How about a scar?"

"That I can do."

After the scar came a scraggly beard and an oily rag for a headband. Mike looked in the hand mirror and saw himself transformed. "I look like a hippie," he said.

"You'll do," said Mrs. Range. "Next!"

If there was any consolation, it was that Jin Kim looked even more ridiculous. The mothers had fitted him out with a dirty blond wig, which he ditched backstage the first chance he got.

"Let's break a leg, guys," Mr. Jenkins said, clapping his hands. "Curtain in five minutes!"

"*Alamak!*" said Jin Kim. "Don't wait to crucify. Just kill me now."

There was actually no curtain to speak of. But when the lights went down, Mike took his position in the wings. A hush fell over the amphitheater as the audience took their seats. Somebody coughed. Out of the electric dark, Shep's guitar twanged a melancholy whine…

Afterwards, they changed back into their school uniforms but kept their beards on. It was funny for a while, the way the old aunties at the bus stop gave them scandalized looks. But then Jin Kim's bus came, and Mike was left alone, feeling stupid and *ang moh*.

The sky was dark with rain clouds when the bus left him at the stop on Ferrer Road. He wasn't thinking at all about Mr. Keen then. But he noticed that the Soda Pop Man was still open for business on the other side of the street. And he had a customer.

The Mustang parked in the lay-by was blue instead of red, and the license plate, too, had been changed. But even from this side of the road Mike recognized the arm dangling halfway out the window, a green dragon snaking out of its shirtsleeve.

Ignoring the Mustang, Mike headed straight for the Soda Pop Man's stall, pausing on the traffic island to let a gang of motor scooters pass. "How much is a Coke?"

"No more already," said the Soda Pop Man. "Grape and orange got."

"Okay, grape then. How much?"

"For you, very special price. Two dollar."

"Are you kidding?" said Mike. "Last time it was *one* dollar."

"Price go up," said the Soda Pop Man sadly, turning his palms to the sky. "Inflation very bad, lah."

Mike fished a crumpled bill from his pocket. "This is all I have."

"Okay, this last time. Special for you." The Soda Pop Man stuffed the dollar into a coffee can and flipped open the ice chest. He performed his usual ritual with lightning speed.

Mike didn't approach the Mustang. He didn't even look at it. Instead he leaned against the big tree, in plain view of passing traffic, sucking grape soda through a straw. It must have been a full minute before he heard the Mustang's door open.

"Get in the car, Mike," said Jason Keen. He was on the other side of the car, cradling his arms on top of the canvas roof. He looked like he hadn't shaved or slept in days. Even in shadow, his face glistened with sweat, his eyes feverish and hunted. "We've got to talk."

Mike snorted, grape fizz leaking out his nose. "I'm not getting in any car with *you.*"

"Have you been talking to the colonel?"

"I know it was you," said Mike. "You stole my tiger!"

Mr. Keen's eyes flitted left and right. He took his hands off the car roof and trapped them under his armpits, as if to keep them from flying away. "Okay. Yes, I did. I stole your tiger."

144

"Why?"

"You know why. The intel on that microfilm was toxic. Sooner or later someone was going to kill you for it."

Thunder rolled across the sky.

"She meant it for *me*," said Mike.

"She wouldn't have wanted you dead." Mr. Keen's hands broke free again, like dove wings, as he edged around the car. "It's not safe for you here anymore, Mike. We've got to get you out."

Mike backed away, putting the tree between them. "You lied to me the whole time! All you ever cared about was the microfilm."

Big drops of water were falling. The Soda Pop Man caught one in his upturned hand and peered at the sky.

"That's not true," said Mr. Keen. "Okay, maybe I did lie to you. But this part isn't a lie. This is the part where I get you home safe."

"I saw what's on the microfilm," said Mike. "We're not the good guys."

The Soda Pop Man caught another raindrop, then popped open an umbrella made of waxed paper and wood.

"There are two plane tickets in the car," said Mr. Keen. "A new passport for you. We can make the flight to Tokyo tonight. You could be in Oklahoma in time for church Sunday."

Mike scrunched the plastic baggie in his fist, taking another step back. "I *told* you, I'm not getting in your stupid car. I know all about you."

"Maybe you don't know everything," said Mr. Keen. "Let me help you. Please."

"Give it back first."

"What?"

"Give back what you took!"

"You know I can't do that."

"Why? What are you going to do with it?"

Mr. Keen's shoulders slumped. "I don't know, Mike. We can decide that together. First, let's get you home."

"They're coming back for me. As soon as they finish their undercover work."

Mr. Keen closed his eyes. When he spoke again, his voice sounded tired. "It's been months, Mike. After all this time, don't you think they would have—"

"Shut up!" Mike shouted, ripping fake whiskers from his chin. "You don't know God. You don't have faith the size of a—" He couldn't say anything more. The *feelings* had come back, choking him. "Just stay away from me!"

Then the rain came.

In the sudden downpour he stood at the road's edge, waiting for a break in the traffic. In seconds his clothes were drenched, his made-up face smeared into a Halloween mask. He leapt into the deluge.

Chapter 34

They crucified Jin Kim on Friday. In dress rehearsal the special effects had not been this realistic. Mike, killed off in a previous scene, could only watch from his place of shame in the wings. With every pound of the hammer, he flinched.

In silence they raised Jin Kim up, his slender body transfixed in the spotlight, a rag draped around his hips. His narrow chest heaved. *"My God, my God, why have you forgotten me?"*

There would be no resurrection. Only a slow dimming of lights as the band softly played; then the curtain call, the audience going bananas, howls of rapture from fifth-grade groupies as Jesus and Judas emerged from opposite wings to take their bow.

"Rock stars now, is it?" said Mr. Chen at the reception afterwards. "This boy so eksi one already, how can?" He gave his son a playful cuff, which Jin Kim dodged too late, pulling a face.

Jin Kim's family had turned out in multitudes, only to be outdone by Mrs. Watkins, who brought the whole hostel with her. Mike's face hurt from grinning so much. A sugar high of Coke and cookies had sent him into orbit. He was jumpy and jerky, and found himself running through the halls with a herd of wild children. The school grounds were empty and wide open.

"Let's play sardines!" said Ming.

"Jesus is It," said Krisda. "Everybody gotta find Jesus."

Jin Kim scowled, but dutifully scampered off while they all covered their eyes. Patrick counted to a hundred in Malay, just to show off. After he got to *seratus*, they all stood blinking at each other like newborn foals.

"Coming, ready or not!" Bryan shouted, and they scattered. Mike took off downstairs and made for Mr. Ho's open-air cafeteria. The kitchen was shuttered, but there were still plenty of hiding places in the sprawling seating area. Mike checked under every table, and in each of the little garden plots that grew around the edges. Jin Kim wasn't anywhere.

Mike started to panic. It was a big school, and nobody had set any boundaries. As usual, everything was *bo cheng hu*. The silence gnawed at his nerves, sang in his ears like crickets. Minutes passed in which he saw no sign of Jin Kim or anyone else. Until at last he heard a sound that told him he was not alone. From the parking lot, a distant buzz of motor scooters.

Mike assumed it was just some kids from the local high school showing off. He started up the stairs to continue his search on Level 2, when the buzz exploded into a head-splitting whine. A pair of motor scooters zipped along the walkway below. They skidded around a pillar and stopped, engines revving. Mike raised a hand to shade his eyes from the headlight beams. One of the riders spotted him, and pointed. Then, impossibly, the scooters started climbing the stairs after him, caterwauling as they bounced up the steps.

Mike loped toward the top landing, taking the steps two at a time. It hadn't yet occurred to him that he had become prey. Right now, he just wanted to get out of the way.

But as he reached the top step and lunged to the right, his pursuers wheeled ninety degrees, tires screaming like demonic babies. Mike caught a whiff of smoking rubber as he sprinted past the library. He hadn't really thought of where he was running to. He hadn't really thought at all.

He skidded around the next corner, arms gyrating to hold his balance. At the other end of the walkway, four young riders sat astride their mounts, dressed in blue jeans and snug-fitting shirts. They revved their engines. One of the scooters lurched forward, braking to a stop within a few yards of Mike. A pair of sunglasses concealed the rider's eyes. He sprouted a steely blade from his hand, twisting it gently to catch the light so it gleamed.

And I looked, and behold a pale horse: and his name that sat on him was Death, and Hell followed with him. Mike whirled around, only to find two more scooters behind him. His pursuers had cut off his escape. There was nowhere to run.

"Boy. You come with us now."

Mike slowly shook his head. His feet slid into a fighting stance.

The lead rider held Mike in the reflective shields of his sunglasses. His lips twisted into a smile. He said something in Hokkien, and the others laughed. Abruptly he raised a hand in the air and snapped his fingers. One of the motor scooters broke formation and charged.

The tires squealed in a burst of speed, the front wheel popping into the air like a stallion rearing. Mike held his ground until the last second, then stepped nimbly to the side and caught the rider in the ribs with a simple side kick. It was enough. Rider and machine separated in a slow-motion ballet. The scooter hit the ground and spun like a whirligig across the tiles, leaving a trail of sparks. A few yards away, the unhorsed rider staggered to his feet in a daze.

This time nobody was smiling. The lead rider raised his arms and thrust both hands forward. Two scooters peeled off this time, buzzing past their leader on either side before exploding in a burst of speed. Mike chose his target. He feinted left, then pivoted into a roundhouse kick, slamming the rider into his companion. The boys landed in a heap, their scooters flying out from under them. The machines continued their trajectory for several yards more, metal screeching against tile, until their engines sputtered and died. Smells of burning rubber and leaking gasoline lingered in the stagnant air.

It was not yet over. The lead rider revved his engine, his face warping into a snarl. Mike made ready to meet his last attacker, but he had forgotten to look behind. Something solid and heavy hit him in the back, and the floor flew up to meet his face. He cried out, but lost his breath when a knee landed in the center of his spine. He kicked his legs uselessly. Something wet and toxic pressed against his mouth and nose, muffling his scream.

"You come with us now."

Rainbow colors lifted him, swirling, and carried him into the dark.

Chapter 35

He woke to the hum of an engine, water rippling against wood; smells of dead fish and seaweed and mildew. He peeled his face off a vinyl mattress and retched into a coil of wet rope.

The cramped V-shaped room was bouncing around. A spray of mist hit him in the face. He looked up and saw a hatch above his head, half-open to the sky.

Mike scrambled to his knees and pushed upwards on the hatch. Wind and spray licked his face. The sky was overcast, and a loose tail of rope whipped the deck. The boat thudded wave to wave, alone on a choppy sea.

Mike sank back down and clutched his knees. The hatch clapped shut above his head, and he winced. His kidnappers would know he was awake now. He had to act fast.

He scooted down off the berth, hunted among the piles of equipment for something he could use as a weapon. His hands moved quicker as his panic grew. Life jackets, bungie cords, signal flags, rope, fishing tackle. From out of that mess he dug a rusty wrench, and tested the weight in his hand.

He hoisted himself back onto the berth and gently pushed on the hatch. It opened a couple of inches, and he paused, waiting for an angry voice to raise the alarm. Hearing only wind and waves, he opened it a fraction more, then far enough to poke his head and shoulders through. A wooden deck narrowed toward the bow, and behind him stood a mast with a furled sail. Clutching the wrench, he wriggled the rest of the way through, scraping his legs against the steel lip of the hatch. He tumbled onto the deck with a soft thud. He lay still for a minute, though it seemed a much longer time, pressing his cheek into the weathered wood. Still there was no angry shout, no sounding of alarm. Only the sea and the wind, and the engine's monotonous hum.

But *someone* was back there, maybe even a whole crew. If it was just one guy, he stood a chance, but any more than that... Mike's fingers tightened around the wrench.

He pushed slowly against the deck with both hands, lifting himself just high enough to see over the top of the cabin into the cockpit beyond. He spotted a man's hand holding a chrome steering wheel. Mike crept closer, peering around the base of the mast. He couldn't see the man's face, but he didn't need to. The tattoo dragon creeping down the forearm was enough.

"Hey there, buddy," said Jason Keen. "Feeling better?"

Mike felt dizzy as he stood up. He staggered to the starboard shrouds and held on. The boat rolled over the crest of a wave and crashed into the trough, sending a whiplash of spray across his back. He tightened his grip on the shroud and lifted the wrench shoulder-high in his other hand, like a sword. He didn't say anything. He couldn't. The feelings had all come together in his throat, tightening into a lump. All he could do was hold on.

"If you plan on braining me with that thing," said Mr. Keen, "now's your chance." He turned his eyes back to the horizon, holding the helm one-handed.

Mike studied the rusty wrench at arm's length, as if he didn't know how it had got into his hand. He would never be able to hit anybody with it. Not even a dangerous kidnapper like Mr. Keen.

The boat plowed into another wave, and Mike fumbled, hugging the shrouds with both arms. His weapon dropped into the roiling sea with barely a splash.

"I'm sorry we had to do it this way," said Mr. Keen. "The boys didn't hurt you, did they?" He chuckled. "You certainly made an impression on *them*."

Mike lifted his leg over the guardrail and straddled it, searching the horizon for land. All he saw was water. There was no way to judge the distance to shore. Was it a mile? Ten miles? He lifted his other leg over the guardrail, balancing both feet on the edge of the deck, gripping the shrouds tightly as he looked down. The foamy water was a blur beneath his sneakers. His knees were shaking.

"You can't swim it, Mike," said Mr. Keen. "It's too far."

Mike stayed where he was, not on the boat and not off it, just hanging on. "Don't come near me," he said.

Mr. Keen raised one hand, as if in half-surrender. "Come back inside the guardrails, Mike."

"I'm not taking orders from a kidnapper!"

Mr. Keen winced. "I know how this looks, but you didn't give me much choice. It's the only way I could get you out."

"When my dad comes back for me, he's going to kill you."

"Okay," said Mr. Keen. "But until then, can we lay some ground rules? You're going to stay inside the guardrails. There's a life jacket down below that you're going to put on. I brought some clean clothes for you, as well."

Mike didn't move. He would not obey a kidnapper. He had taken a stand, and he could not back down, even if part of him wished he could. It would be better to drown.

"Mike," said Mr. Keen, his voice commanding. "Inside the guardrails. Life jacket. Now."

Mike stared at the frothing water under his feet. He shook his head.

"Yes, you can."

"No, I can't!"

He teetered in the face of the wind, holding on, until the wire shrouds cut deep grooves into his hands. In the end, he didn't resist as Mr. Keen's voice guided him down into the cockpit, one step at a time. There was no other voice but his.

"Life jacket," said Mr. Keen.

"But *you're* not wearing one," said Mike.

"Captain's prerogative."

A sudden weariness came over him. He had to go down the steps backwards to get into the cabin, clutching at the handrails on either side of the main hatch. Down here the roar of the engine was louder, vibrating through the floor. The air smelled of salt water and diesel and mildew.

On the starboard berth he found a pile of moldy life jackets. Most of them were too big, but he picked the closest fit and put it on. It was bulky and uncomfortable and smelled like stale sweat. He cinched the nylon belt and grabbed another life jacket off the pile before starting up the steps.

When Mike climbed through the main hatch into the cockpit, he held the extra life jacket at arm's length toward Mr. Keen, careful to keep a safe distance between himself and the kidnapper.

Mr. Keen looked at him in surprise.

"First mate's prerogative," said Mike. "If I have to wear one, so do you."

Mr. Keen looked away to the horizon, then looked back at Mike, as if calculating all the different ways a boy could make his life difficult. "Fine," he said, snatching the life jacket out of Mike's hand.

Mike 1, Kidnapper 0.

"Don't think this is because I care if you drown," said Mike. "Because I don't."

"Take the helm," said Mr. Keen, scooting over on the bench.

Mike looked at him warily. "Why?"

"Because I asked you to," said Mr. Keen. "Keep the same bearing for now."

"Where are we?" Mike slid into the helmsman's seat. He felt the vibration of the engine through his hands as he took the chrome wheel. He stretched his neck to peer at the compass needle in front of him.

"South China Sea, about forty miles northeast of Singapore." Mr. Keen slipped the life jacket over his head and cinched the belt. "We need to put up the sails to save our fuel. Do you think you can steer her into the wind?"

"Um..."

Mr. Keen pointed to a telltale string of yarn fluttering from the starboard shroud. "You see that string? Make it point toward the stern, and keep it there." He reached across Mike's knees to ease the throttle back, and the engine's roar became a steady chug. "Now, point her into the wind."

Mike turned the wheel, keeping his eye on the telltale until it pointed directly to the rear. Mr. Keen climbed out of the cockpit and made his way to the mast. He unhitched the main halyard rope and pulled. The mainsail climbed the mast in jumps and starts, flapping in the wind. He wrapped the halyard rope around the winch and cranked it tight. Then he inched his way around to the other side of the mast and grabbed another rope. A second, smaller sail rose flapping up the forestay. Its sheet-ropes whipped the deck as Mr. Keen crawled back into the cockpit.

"Ease her to starboard," said Mr. Keen.

"What?"

"Turn right, but slow. Take her to north-northwest."

Mike turned the wheel until the bow swung right. The boat tilted sideways, and the sails stopped flapping as they caught the wind. Mike felt a new tautness in the helm, the hull racing through water.

Mr. Keen adjusted the mainsail, letting the boom out a little. He pulled on another rope, cranking it through the winch, until the jib was firm and trim. Then he reached over Mike's knees again and pulled the throttle all the way back. The engine sputtered and died.

Almost instantly, a kind of peace settled over them. The only sounds were of wind and sea. Water tickling the hull, waves splashing the bow. The steady, noiseless hum of sail.

Mr. Keen leaned over to check the compass. He lifted a hand to pat Mike's shoulder, but then seemed to change his mind. The hand went back to his side. "Hold her steady a while. I need to catch some shuteye." He started down the steps of the main hatch.

"Wait," said Mike. "You're just gonna leave me here?"

"You have the helm," Mr. Keen said over his shoulder. He ducked under the hatch and disappeared.

You have the helm. As if that even meant anything. He had control of the boat but didn't know where they were going. There was no hint of land anywhere. He thought of waiting until his kidnapper was asleep and then tying him up with bungie cords. But then what? Mr. Keen was the only one who could get them safely to shore. For now, Mike would have to act the part. He would obey in word and action, but not in his heart. As soon as they got safely to land, he would escape.

Making the decision took some of the pressure off, and Mike felt a lightening in his shoulders. Here he was, steering the boat, while the so-called adult was asleep below! He had the helm; he was in charge. Through his hands he felt the thrumming of the sails and the immense power of the sea.

Chapter 36

Two hours later he was still steering. His back and shoulders were beginning to ache from the strain of holding the boat on course. A few times he had almost dozed off, and now he forced himself to steer standing up, to stay awake. Off the starboard bow some dark smudges of cloud were gathering, but he didn't pay them any mind at first. Then the wind changed direction, and the sails ruffled. "Mr. Keen?"

A sudden gust came from starboard, and the boom snapped leeward. The sails flipped to catch the new alien wind. Mike struggled at the helm to keep her steady. The boat tilted dangerously, gathering speed. Water raced along the gunwales. "Mr. Keen!"

Down below, pots and pans and cans of food clattered to the floor and rolled around. Mr. Keen's sleepy face appeared at the hatch. "Put her into the wind, Mike!" He started to climb the steps, but the bow crashed into a wave, and he flew backwards down the hatch.

"Mr. Keen!"

Mike looked for the telltale string of yarn and pulled the wheel to starboard. Slowly the boat began to turn, easing out of her dangerous tilt. Now she danced precariously on the crests of waves, sails flapping wild. Mike reached for the ignition key and turned it. The engine sputtered to life.

Wind whistled through the stays. The boat rose and crashed over a steep swell, and Mike struggled to keep her nose into the wind. He pushed on the throttle to give her some speed, and the engine hummed.

"Mr. Keen!"

The boat pitched as she rode over a wave as high as a house. Mike felt his guts left up in the air as she crashed downward into the trough with a huge splash. A cascade of salt water fell like rain, drenching

Mike's clothes and hair and face. Still Mr. Keen hadn't answered. Mike imagined him knocked out below, or lying dead under a pile of debris. He felt a stinging in his eyes, but couldn't tell if it was from salt water or from tears.

"Hold her steady!" a voice called from below. Mr. Keen's face appeared again at the main hatch. He clambered up the steps and tumbled into the cockpit as the boat hit another high swell. Water crashed over the gunwales. Mr. Keen staggered to his feet and climbed onto the cabin roof. On hands and knees, he crawled toward the mast.

Mike held onto the wheel, the only thing that kept him from flying overboard as the boat pitched and rolled. Wind sang through the wire stays and howled in his ears. He clenched his jaw to stop his teeth chattering, but he couldn't stop his body from shaking. He tightened his grip on the wheel as the bow rose to meet another swell.

The boat came down again with a crash. Mr. Keen lay prone on the cabin roof, hugging the base of the mast. He untied the main halyard rope and started pulling the mainsail down, grabbing at the sailcloth with his bare hands.

The sky had grown darker. Lightning struck the sea, and the rain came down. Water fell at Mike from all sides, up and down and sideways, whipping his face and arms and legs until his skin felt like it was being sandpapered off.

Mr. Keen was still stumbling around on the cabin roof. He secured the mainsail to the boom with bungie cords, then moved on to the jib. When he finally crawled back into the cockpit, his hair was plastered to his scalp, water streaming down his chin like a liquid beard. He staggered as the boat pitched, then reached for the wheel. "Get below, Mike!" he shouted.

Mike sat down, one hand on the guardrail, the other hand gripping the edge of the bench.

"Mike, get below, now!"

"No, sir!" Mike screamed back. "What if you go overboard?"

Mr. Keen swore. Mike shook his head.

"In the cabin there's a harness and lifeline," Mr. Keen shouted. "Can you get it for me?"

Mike stumbled to the main hatch and grabbed the handrails, easing himself down one step at a time. The boat pitched high and slammed into a trough, throwing Mike backwards. He landed on the narrow cabin floor, sprawling among cans of Campbell's soup and *chili con carne* with beans.

"Under the chart table!"

He crawled on hands and knees amid the rolling cans. Under a foldaway table he found the nylon harness with the long coil of rope attached. It looked like something you would put on a horse.

When Mike came back through the hatch, Mr. Keen was spinning the wheel wildly, as wave after wave knocked the boat off its course. Mike fell onto the bench and scooted toward Mr. Keen with the harness in hand. The kidnapper grabbed him by the arm and hauled him behind the wheel. "Take her!" he shouted. "You have the helm."

Mike grabbed the wheel with both hands as Mr. Keen slipped the harness on. A wave hit the hull almost broadside, and the boat pitched sideways. Mike spun the wheel to port, turning the bow to catch the waves head-on.

Mr. Keen tightened his harness and slid forward on the bench. He attached the rope to the guardrail with a snap hook and inched his way back. He grabbed Mike's arm and shouted in his ear. "There. I'm secured. Now get below deck and stay there!"

Mr. Keen took the wheel, and Mike staggered into the maelstrom of rain and spray. He climbed backwards down the main hatch and stopped halfway down the steps, holding on to the handrails and watching the furious battle outside. Mr. Keen stood behind the wheel, blinking into the rain, as waves crashed over the gunwales. Any minute he could be blown over the side. Mike tossed up a prayer: *Don't leave me alone.*

Hours later, Mr. Keen was still there. Mike couldn't remember at what point he knew they were going to be safe. Neither could he be certain he wasn't dreaming when he saw Jesus come walking down the long face of a wave. He only knew that sometime in the night the storm relented. The wind screamed less shrilly than before, the waves' fury slackened, and the boat's wild death-dance became manageable.

Mike was suddenly overcome with tiredness. He thought he might fall asleep where he was standing. He barely made it to the berth before his eyes closed.

He woke with a sense of shame for having slept—for leaving his captain to battle the storm alone. But when he climbed into the cockpit, he found Mr. Keen grinning like a boy who has played king-of-the-hill and won. "Wild ride last night, eh, Mike?"

Mike looked around. The boat chugged happily across a glassy sea. The sky in the east had lightened, and up ahead, a thin strip of land was visible on the horizon. He could see structures along the sea's edge that looked like houses.

Mike felt the dampness of his clothes, and shivered.

"You'd better dry off," said Mr. Keen. "There's a duffel bag down below with some clean clothes for you."

"I'm fine," said Mike, his teeth chattering. He had to start planning now. Soon they would be ashore, and he would have to make his escape.

"Mike," said Mr. Keen, his voice firm. "Go below and get changed."

Mike did as he was told. For now.

Below deck he peeled off his wet clothes and took a minute hunting through the jumble on the floor. It was the tiger he spotted first, poking his head through the duffel bag's zipper. "Charlie?"

The tiger seemed to smile at him with his glass-button eyes. Mike pulled him out of the duffel bag and explored the furry body with his fingers, pressing into the soft underbelly with his thumbs. He felt the edge of something solid. A reel? He looked closer at the stitching. Someone had taken the trouble to re-sew the tiger's head properly with the right color thread.

Mike glanced up through the main hatch. All that was visible of Mr. Keen was his left foot. A Dockers boat shoe. No socks.

Mike found a clean pair of shorts and a T-shirt inside the bag and put them on. It felt good to be dry. He put Charlie back into the duffel with his dirty clothes and stowed the bag where he would remember to find it later. Then he started cleaning up the mess in the cabin, shepherding the stray cans of soup, returning the pots and pans to their proper places on the galley shelves. It was a chore he didn't have time to finish. His captain was calling him.

"Mike, get up here!"

Chapter 37

The inlet was well protected, the hotel on the beach barely visible from the sea. An open-air restaurant with a thatched roof nestled among a cluster of weather-beaten shacks. They were the only guests.

The hotel launch had come out to meet them where they had anchored, and let them off on a creaky wooden pier. There was no reception desk to check in at, but Mr. Keen seemed to know where he was going. Mike slung the duffel over his shoulder and followed. At the far end of the beach they came to a dilapidated cabin. The door was open. Mr. Keen kicked off his boat shoes and collapsed onto the nearest bed, without saying another word.

Mike perched on the edge of the other bed, the strap of the duffel still tight across his shoulder. He had planned to wait until Mr. Keen was asleep and then make his getaway. But his eyes were heavy, and he thought it wouldn't hurt to rest them a little. He leaned back on the mattress, keeping his feet on the floor, the duffel bag firmly at his side. Just a few minutes was all he needed.

When he woke, the late afternoon sun was streaming in through the grimy window above his head. He sat up fast, his head spinning, and took a sharp breath. The other bed was empty. He had waited too long. He had to move *now*.

He shouldered the duffel bag and jumped to his feet, but didn't quite make it to the door. Mr. Keen emerged from the bathroom, rubbing his wet hair with a towel. "Going somewhere?" he said.

Mike clutched the duffel bag close to his side. "I just wanted to explore a little."

"You can leave the bag. Nobody's going to steal it here."

"I need it," said Mike, "in case I find something."

"Like what?"

Mike shrugged. "I don't know. Shells."

Mr. Keen snorted. "Take a shower, first. You stink."

"I'll take one later."

Mr. Keen frowned at him. "What's wrong with you? You can't go to dinner like that."

"Dinner?"

"They're laying on a spread for us. Don't embarrass me."

Mike clenched his teeth, eyeing the door. Soon it would be dark, and too late to run.

"You're not going anywhere," said Mr. Keen. "Not until after you've showered."

"Fine," said Mike, stamping into the bathroom. He flung the duffel bag onto the wet floor and slammed the door. Then locked it.

From the dingy mirror, a boy looked back at him, chiseled and lean, with eyes that held a fierceness in them. What if his parents didn't recognize him when he got home?

The shower was cold. He cringed under the water, taking quick gasps of air, and came out shaking. There were no more fresh clothes in the duffel, so he put on the same shorts and T-shirt he'd had on before. He didn't bother with shoes.

Once outside, he waited for Mr. Keen to say something about his bare feet, but the kidnapper didn't even notice. They were silent as they trekked down the beach, the sun sinking below the trees. Mike took a detour to the water, playing tag with the waves, until Mr. Keen called him back. His feet were coated in wet sand as they stepped into the restaurant.

They were the only customers. Mr. Keen picked a table looking out at the sea. A waiter came and asked them what they wanted to drink. "I'll have the usual," Mr. Keen said, and Mike made a mental note. The kidnapper had been here before. He was, in fact, a regular customer.

"Isn't he going to bring us some menus?" asked Mike, after the waiter had brought their drinks.

"There's no menu," said Mr. Keen. "Dinner is whatever's in today's catch."

"But what if it's something gross, like boiled octopus? Or jellyfish salad? Or—"

"We'll eat it. Whatever they put on the table."

Mike slurped his Coke. "Where are we, anyway?" He tried to make it sound like a casual question.

Mr. Keen slapped at a mosquito and checked his hand for the corpse. "Can you do the math?"

Mike calculated. "Forty miles northeast, then north-northwest. We're in Malaysia, right?"

"Bingo," said Mr. Keen. "We'll make a sailor of you, yet."

Mike smiled. It was okay to smile, because that put Mr. Keen at ease, and the more at ease he was, the less alert he would be. Mike would make his move when the kidnapper least expected it.

"We're safe here," Mr. Keen was saying. "There's no road to speak of. The only practical way in or out is by sea."

The waiter came back. "Mister Jason. Phone call for you."

Mr. Keen took a quick gulp of his cocktail before standing up. "I'll be right back." He followed the waiter to the bar and lifted a telephone to his ear.

Mike glanced at Mr. Keen's half-empty glass and wondered how many of those orangey cocktails it would take to get him drunk. He knew it was technically a sin, but he had to know. He slid the glass over, keeping a wary eye on the bar, and lifted it to his lips.

He almost choked in surprise. The so-called cocktail was pure papaya juice.

He quickly set the glass down again in its little puddle of dew. Mr. Keen was hanging up the phone. Mike wiped the streak marks off the table with a napkin.

"Who was that?" he asked innocently.

Mr. Keen sat down again and picked up his drink. "That was my associate," he said. "It shouldn't be long now."

"What do you mean? Who's your associate?"

Just then the waiter returned, carrying a large roasted fish on a platter. He set it in the middle of the table and placed a ceramic plate in front of each of them. The fish was lying on its belly and still had its head on. The mouth was hanging open, and the eyes looked at Mike with a surprised expression.

He reached over and turned the platter around so the fish faced Mr. Keen.

The kidnapper gave him a severe look.

"What?" said Mike. "The fish was staring at me."

"Anything else?" said the waiter.

Mr. Keen drained his glass and set it down on the table. "Better bring me another one of these," he said.

Mike wasn't fooled. Mr. Keen had been pretending all this time to be some kind of drunk, but it was just an act. Mike wondered what other lies Mr. Keen had been feeding him.

"What about my parents?" said Mike. He spooned some of the roast potatoes from the platter onto his plate. He didn't touch the fish. "When are you going to tell me where they are?" He picked up his fork and waited.

Mr. Keen pushed a forkful of fish into his mouth and chewed it slowly, as if he needed time to think up a good enough lie.

"They're dead, aren't they," Mike answered for him.

When he said it, something in his heart died, as if he had stabbed it with his dinner knife. He felt like a murderer. The words hung in the air between them like storm clouds waiting to explode into rain.

Mr. Keen paused with another forkful of fish halfway to his mouth. He lowered the fork slowly and laid it on his plate. He glanced at Mike, but quickly dropped his gaze. His voice was barely a murmur when he said: "The official word is Missing."

"Missing. What does that even *mean?*"

Mr. Keen couldn't look at Mike for more than a second. "It means no bodies were found. Missing... and Presumed Dead."

"Presumed?" The word sounded old-fashioned and silly, like someone had lifted it out of a thesaurus. Mike pictured some 19th century guy in a safari suit with a big mustache. *Dr. Livingstone, I presume.*

They had both stopped eating.

"Why didn't someone tell me?" said Mike. Then, his voice wavering: "Why didn't *you* tell me?"

Mr. Keen looked down at his plate. The fish stared out at the darkling sea with the same surprised look on its face.

"Excuse me," said Mike. He stood up. He pushed his chair in. He was being polite, like his parents always wanted him to be. As if there was anyone left to care. He tramped down the wooden steps to the beach. He walked until he could feel the wet sand under his feet, the cold undertow of waves streaming back to the sea.

Chapter 38

Sunlight blazed through a smeary window. With a start, Mike remembered he was supposed to be escaping. He sat up and wiped the sleep from his eyes. On the other side of the room, Mr. Keen's bed was empty and made.

Mike searched under his bed for the duffel bag and unzipped it. The tiger was still there, but all his clothes were gone. Even the ones he'd worn yesterday had been taken from the chair where he had left them. In their place he found an old pair of shorts that must have belonged to some other boy. The fabric was faded and fraying at the seams. There was no shirt or socks or shoes.

Whoever had stolen his clothes must think it was some kind of joke. Or maybe he was being punished. It didn't matter. If Mr. Keen thought this would stop him from running away, he had another think coming. The shorts, at least, were clean. He didn't have anything else to wear, so he put them on.

The duffel was light and the sun warm on his bare shoulders as he walked down the beach. He passed the restaurant and saw Mr. Keen sitting at the same table as the night before. Mr. Keen waved to him, but Mike didn't wave back. He walked to the far end of the beach and clambered over a cluster of half-submerged rocks. On the other side he found only water, waves lapping languidly into a patch of mangroves. There was no way through.

The rocks bit into his bare feet as he traced his way back to the beach. He scanned the line of trees where jungle met sand, but couldn't find any path or opening. Maybe Mr. Keen had been telling the truth for once: the only way in or out was by sea.

Mike kicked sand at a hermit crab and watched it scuttle back into its hole. There was no way out. He leaned against a palm tree and slid down into the sand, burying his head in his arms. The waves made a peaceful sound, but it was all a lie. Mike was a prisoner here. The sea was his warden, and the jungle was an impenetrable wall. *You'll never leave,* whispered the waves, and the palm trees nodded their shaggy heads as if they agreed.

Further down the beach, a boy was lugging a basket full of fruit. Mike watched him, wondering where he had come from. The basket was a big one, and the boy had to set it down and pick it up a few times before he made it to the restaurant.

Mike stood up slowly. He ran in a crouch toward the forest's edge and ducked behind a plant with big leaves. From his new hiding place, he could see the boy standing next to his basket in the shade of the restaurant's thatched roof. A man came out of the shadows and started poking around in the basket—papayas, mangos, rambutans—while the boy balanced on one foot and then the other. They seemed to be negotiating.

The boy pocketed some money and turned back. Mike lay flat, pressing his belly into the prickly sand. He watched through a mesh of weeds as the boy approached along the jungle's edge and then disappeared. *There.* Mike jumped up and ran to the place where the boy had gone. A sandy footpath led into the forest. He could see the boy's fresh footprints. Further down the path, a movement among the trees. He waited a few seconds before following.

It was shaded and cool in the forest. Speckles of sunlight brushed the ground with gold. Mike crouched low as he crept along the sandy trail, trying to stay close enough to the boy so he wouldn't lose him. But he was already falling behind. Brittle pieces of leaves and twigs bit into his feet, and he wished he had shoes. The other boy was barefoot too, but he quickly outpaced Mike, disappearing into the dense foliage. For a minute Mike stood alone, breathing hard, trying to think what to do. He could turn back, but then he might never find out where the trail led to. This might be his only chance.

He continued on until the path opened into a clearing. A row of stilted houses stretched out along the shore. The boy was leaning against a palm tree at the trail's end, waiting for him. Mike froze in his tracks and stared.

"*Datang*," the boy said in Malay. He beckoned. "Come."

Fighting his shyness, Mike jogged to catch up. "Hi," he said.

The boy answered with a flood of gibberish. Mike wished he had paid more attention in Malay class.

Maybe there was some adult in the kampong he could talk to. Somebody who spoke English. Somebody who would understand. He scoured his memory for the words in Malay, and found them: "*Di manakah orang dewasa?*" Where are the grown-ups?

The boy laughed, showing a gap between his front teeth. Another flood of Malay. Mike caught a word here and there and pieced together what he could:

The boy's name was Samsam. His father was out fishing, and his mother was working at the hotel.

Soon they were joined by others. Boys of different sizes and ages, all dressed more or less the same: shorts, no shirt, no shoes. One of the littler ones grabbed Mike by the hand and pulled him down the beach. Another wrapped himself around Mike's leg and wouldn't let go until Samsam shooed him away. They were all laughing. Somebody produced a plastic soccer ball, and they started kicking it around. There was an argument about where the goalposts should be. Pieces of drift-wood were moved and put back again. The game started in a kind of anarchy, with no one bothering to pick teams.

Mike still wore the duffel bag on his shoulder, clutching it tight to his side as he chased the ball. A kid pointed at Mike and said something, and everybody laughed. The game paused. Samsam picked up the ball and approached Mike. He pointed at the duffel bag and said something in Malay, then tugged gently at the carrying strap. Mike tugged back. "It's mine," he said.

More laughter. Fingers pointed at Mike, and some of the boys started squabbling. Then a girl appeared, walking down from one of the stilted houses. She was skinny and had serious eyes. She said something to the gaggle of boys which seemed to calm them down. Then she looked at Mike with a patient smile. Her hand touched the carrying strap, but she didn't pull on it yet. She was waiting for Mike to let go, and finally he did, surrendering the last of everything.

He stood watching her go, taking the duffel bag with her. Around him, the game had already resumed. The plastic ball slapped him on the chest, and he caught it with his foot as it fell. He didn't know which team he was on, so he dribbled the ball toward the nearest goal, until a small wiry kid stole it from between his legs. Mike turned and gave chase. He wasn't a great soccer player, but at least he was fast. He headed the kid off before he could score, and kicked the ball out of bounds. Except there *was* no out of bounds. Nobody had bothered to tell him. The ball bounced into the surf, and everybody went in after it. The frenzy of splashing feet grew into a small riot as boys fought each other for the ball. Mike dashed into the melee, the water up to his knees. Kids shoved him, and he shoved them back. Someone kicked the ball further out, where it floated and bobbed in the waves.

After that, it was all pandemonium. The game was forgotten as boys splashed and dunked each other. Someone finally retrieved the ball, and they used it as a missile, taking turns to peg each other. It stung when it hit. Mike got pegged a lot, until his wet skin was blotchy with red marks.

The sun was already high when he dragged himself out of the surf and collapsed on the sand. Samsam joined him, and they sat for a while drying in the sun, watching the others play. Mike was glad they didn't have to talk.

"*Makan*," said Samsam. He stood up and made an eating gesture with his fingers.

"I have to go," said Mike in the best Malay he could muster. He pointed back to the forest where he had come from.

But Samsam had already taken off down the beach in the opposite direction. Mike hurried to catch up.

"Where are we going?" he said. Maybe Samsam would show him where the road was. If there was a road, he could hitchhike to the nearest town. But it was almost noon already. He had to find his duffel bag and get started, or it would be too late.

Samsam stopped at the base of a tall palm tree and grinned.

"*Kelapa*," he said. Mike tilted his head back and looked where Samsam was pointing: a nest of coconuts twenty feet up.

"You've got to be kidding me," Mike said.

Samsam giggled. His hands were already busy tying the ends of an old rope to make a loop. He twisted the loop into a figure-eight shape and stepped into it like a stirrup. He grinned at Mike once more before leaping onto the tree.

Mike could only gape as he watched: Samsam gripped the trunk with his hands and pushed with his feet, scampering up the tree like Spiderman. In another minute it was raining coconuts. Mike gathered them one by one as they thudded onto the sand. He stacked them into a pyramid-shaped pile.

Samsam was a little slower climbing down. He jumped the last six feet and landed gently in the sand. He nodded approvingly at Mike's neat stack of coconuts. Then he took the top one off the pile and smashed it against the tree. A watery liquid spurted out through the cracks. Samsam sucked on the shell, then spat a long stream of juice at Mike through the gap in his teeth.

"Hey!" Mike shoved him.

Samsam laughed, wiping his mouth with the back of his hand. He offered Mike the coconut.

Mike took a long drink, sucking on a crack in the shell. The water was sweet, dribbling down his chin as he drank. He burped and gave the coconut back to Samsam, who banged it against the tree again to break the shell in half. He gave one half to Mike, and they spent a few minutes digging and nibbling at the soft white core. Finally Samsam dropped the empty shell to the sand and gathered an armload of coconuts. Mike did the same, hugging the coconuts against his chest as he followed Samsam back down the trail.

The queasy feeling in Mike's stomach got worse as they approached the hotel. He was back where he had started—even worse, he had lost the duffel bag, too.

The boys entered the restaurant through a side entrance and unloaded their coconuts onto the bar. The waiter counted them and paid

Samson two coins from the cash register after some haggling. Samsam kept one of the coins and offered Mike the other.

Mike shook his head. "You did all the Spiderman stuff."

But Samsam kept pushing the coin at him. Mike felt suddenly self-conscious as he took it. The waiter caught Mike's eye and nodded toward the other side of the restaurant. "Father waiting for you."

Mike's heart jumped inside his chest. "My father?"

He turned quickly around, and just as quickly his heart sank. Mr. Keen was sitting at the same table as before, as if he'd never left.

All Mike's shyness suddenly returned. He was back to being a hotel guest again. Samsam would go one way, down the sandy path through the jungle to the kampong; Mike would have to return to his place at the table where Mr. Keen sat nursing his phony cocktail.

"Bye," said Mike, stuffing his hands into his pockets.

Samsam's smile didn't falter. He slapped Mike's shoulder and took off running, the coin held tightly in his hand.

Chapter 39

"She's a beauty, isn't she?" said Mr. Keen. He was gazing out at the sailboat anchored in the bay, the boat they had come in on, the boat that had almost killed them. "She was built at the Cheoy Lee Shipyard in Hong Kong, made to order. Real teak decks. It'll be pity to scuttle her."

Mike slid into a chair at the kidnapper's table, eyeing him sideways. "What are we doing here, Mr. Keen?" he said. "How much longer—"

"Tonight," said Mr. Keen. "She'll come tonight."

"She?"

"My associate." Mr. Keen took a sip from his fake cocktail and looked out at the sea. "She'll take you to Kuala Lumpur, and you'll catch a plane from there. Tokyo, Honolulu, then on to Oklahoma City." His voice sounded as far away as the cities he named.

"And that's it?" said Mike. "After all this, I'm supposed to just—"

"If you run into any trouble, go to the police. The local ones, I mean, not the Feds. Stay away from the Feds."

"So you're *still* not going to tell me?"

Mr. Keen turned his head, his eyes concealed behind mirrored lenses. "What is it you want me to tell you, Mike?"

Mike's lip trembled. He couldn't trust himself to speak. Words were explosive things with lit fuses, and if he chose the wrong one, it might go off.

"Your father isn't a spy, if that's what you're asking," said Mr. Keen. "His job as a diplomat isn't cover. He's the real deal."

"Then why—"

"It's your mother who's the operative."

Mike stared. "But that doesn't make any sense. Dad always has the important job. Mom just does whatever—"

"A fine covert officer, I might add," said Jason Keen. "The best."

Mike struggled to make sense of it, but couldn't comprehend what was impossible to imagine. His whole life was turning into a lie. Maybe it would have been better not to know, but he had to ask— "Does she have anything do with the Phoenix Program?"

Mr. Keen reached for his drink. His hand trembled as he tilted the glass to his mouth. The ice cubes clinked. "There'd been stories going around about the Phoenix Program for years. But hardly anyone knew about its connection to the heroin trade. She was getting ready to blow the whole thing wide open."

"My *mom?*"

"It goes all the way to the top of the South Vietnamese government. The CIA has always looked the other way. Until your mother started snooping around." Mr. Keen snorted. "Except she did more than just snoop. She assembled evidence."

"The microfilm—"

"Yes, the microfilm. But she was smart. She buried the important stuff under a pile of shocking images. The killing, the burning of villages, the torture, all the stuff nobody cared about. The stuff everybody already knew."

"Old news," said Mike, recalling what Mr. Chen had said.

"That's right," said Mr. Keen. "Old news. But buried in that haystack were some hidden jewels. Only someone with the right knowledge could uncover them."

"Someone like you?"

Mr. Keen didn't answer. He caught the waiter's attention and pointed at his empty glass.

"I don't get it," said Mike. "The mission... You *knew* Mr. Chen wasn't a communist? You just made it up?"

"No. Chen was digging around, asking a lot of questions. There were serious concerns about how much he knew."

"But why me?" said Mike, choking up. "Why did you have to pick *me?*"

"I had to keep you close. Find out what you knew. What you might have *on* you."

"So you fed me a bunch of lies about serving my country."

"No. Not lies. You *did* serve."

"Bullshit!"

Mr. Keen took off his sunglasses and pinched the bridge of his nose. His voice trembled when he said, "What do you want me to say, Mike? They were going to send me back. Da Nang. You have no idea what it's like out there. The things I had to do."

"Then at least tell me what you know," said Mike. "I wrote them a million letters, and they never wrote back."

Mr. Keen's hands were shaking as he put his sunglasses back on. The waiter came with a fresh drink and set it on the table, but Mr. Keen didn't touch it. He nudged his sunglasses up and wiped the corner of his eye with a knuckle. "I told you all I know," he said. "It's time for you to get cleaned up."

Mike made a face. "What for?"

"When she comes, there's going to be a celebration. Our wedding anniversary. We're going to be a happy family enjoying a vacation at the beach, and you need to look the part. The dutiful and well-behaved son."

"Are you *kidding* me?"

"Wash your hair, for once. And put on a clean shirt with a collar. And shoes."

Mike stood up quickly, almost knocking his chair over. "Don't you ever get tired of ordering people around?"

Mr. Keen looked at him, unsmiling. "I'm *asking* you," he said. "Don't blow our cover."

Mike rolled his eyes. "*Fine.* But how I am supposed to get changed when somebody stole all my clothes?"

"The girl washed them for you. Check on your bed."

"What girl?" said Mike suspiciously.

But when he got back to the cabin, he found them just like Mr. Keen had said. Clean and neatly folded inside the duffel, with Charlie the tiger sitting on top. As if he was keeping watch.

Chapter 40

She came in the night, standing on the bow of the launch as it cruised into the bay, her black hair streaming in the moonlight, her red evening gown billowing around her stiletto heels. The heels did not slow her down at all as she stepped off the launch onto the weather-beaten pier. For a moment she paused, one hand on her hip, lowering her sunglasses to peer at the moonlit beach where Jason Keen and the boy stood waiting for her.

"Darling," said the Lady of the Night, stepping off the pier into Jason Keen's arms. Mike watched in horror as they entwined in a long kiss, his mouth covering hers, like they were glued together.

Their lips finally came apart with a hideous wet sound. "Happy Anniversary, sweetheart," said Jason Keen. He caught Mike's eye and winked.

"My little boy, so handsome one!" Mike flinched as she snared him in a tight hug, planting a wet kiss on his cheek. The stench of perfume was strong enough to etherize an army of frogs.

"Dressed to kill, as always," said Jason Keen, taking her hand. He pecked her bare shoulder, and she curled her neck back like a contented cat.

The Lady of the Night took off her high heeled shoes, and they walked arm-in-arm up the beach. The boatmen followed with the Lady's bags. Mike took up the rear of the procession like a reluctant altar boy, sweating into his clean white school shirt. It was too late to run.

Spectators had gathered to watch, like visitors at a zoo. They hung by their elbows from the railing that surrounded the restaurant, grinning from the shadows. Mike cringed when he recognized some of the boys from the kampong.

The waiter ushered them to the table closest to the sea. A white table cloth had been laid out, with candles flickering inside little glass jars. Above their heads, a tinsel banner glittered in the electric light: *Happy New Year*, it said.

"Many congratulations," said the waiter. "Something to drink for happy couple?"

After they ordered, the so-called happy couple made a show of holding hands and looking fondly into each other's eyes. Mike subdued an impulse to make barfing noises. He fidgeted with the salt and pepper shakers instead, until the waiter brought him his Coke, and then he fidgeted with that.

"What if I don't *want* to go?" he blurted.

Mr. Keen and the Lady looked at each other.

"My grandparents," said Mike. "They don't even like me. And besides, there's still a chance—"

"Why talk lai dat?" said the Lady of the Night, putting her hand on top of his. She squeezed his fingers until they hurt. "So handsome nice boy, how cannot love you?"

Mike pulled his hand away. "Just drop the phony accent, okay? I know you're American."

Something changed in the Lady's face. Her eyes went hard.

Mr. Keen leaned close and wrapped his fingers around Mike's arm. He whispered fiercely through his teeth: "Do I need to take you back to the room for a *talk*, son?"

"You're not my dad."

"Watch me." Jason Keen tightened his grip.

The scene was being watched from the shadows by a dozen pairs of eyes, and Mike considered playing it out to its end. He could call Mr. Keen's bluff, throw a tantrum, sow enough confusion to cover his getaway. He might even make it as far as the kampong. But then what?

"Neh mind," said the Lady of the Night, waving her hand dismissively. "This bad one not spoil anniversary. Darling, can fetch handbag from room or not?"

"Of course, sweetheart," said Mr. Keen, letting go of Mike's arm. "We could send the boy…"

"No, no," she said. "Mother and son need have chat." She looked at Mike, narrowing her eyes to slits.

"Try not to kill him," said Mr. Keen. His chair legs scraped the floor as he stood up. Mike watched the Hawaiian shirt fade into the night.

The Lady waited until they were alone. Then she glowered at Mike and said: "Where is it?"

"Where's what?"

"You know what I mean."

Mike folded his arms. "I don't have anything to say to you."

"Does *he* have it?"

"I don't know what you're talking about," said Mike.

The Lady closed her lipsticky mouth and breathed hard through her nose. Mike met her stare, one-on-one, until she gave up and sighed. "Listen, maybe we got off on the wrong foot. It seems there's a misunderstanding."

"There's no misunderstanding," said Mike. "You're a liar and a traitor, just like him."

"Oh," she said, as if suddenly comprehending. "You think I'm working with *him*."

Mike, caught off guard, tried not to show his surprise. He kept his mouth closed and waited for her to say more.

"Hon, I'm here on Company business," she said. "The colonel sent me. My job is to get you safely back to Singapore."

"You'll take me back?"

"Of course. That's home for you, isn't it? But first I need to know the whereabouts of a certain item of interest."

Mike looked at her warily, trying to read her face. He didn't know who he could trust anymore. Maybe no one.

"It's safe," he said finally, hedging his bet.

"Safe," she repeated, leaning forward across the table. "Safe where?" She glared at him, and he glared straight back.

"I said it's *safe*."

The Hawaiian shirt reappeared out of the shadows. Mr. Keen set a black sequined handbag on the table and bent down to kiss the Lady on the cheek. "Things seem to have calmed down since I left."

"Darling, you know me," said the Lady of the Night. "I have way with childrens."

Mike scowled.

"That's why I married you," said Mr. Keen, taking her hand and squeezing it. "Such a good mother for my boy."

Oh, good grief, thought Mike. "May I be excused?"

"We haven't eaten yet," said Mr. Keen, frowning. "And besides, there are things we have to discuss."

"Like what?"

Before Mr. Keen could reply, the waiter arrived with a tray of food. It could have been the same fish from the night before, miraculously resurrected. Except that it was dead, of course. Like a zombie fish, it gaped mournfully at Mike from its bed of rice and vegetables.

After dinner, the happy couple danced. A scratchy Barry Manilow record played on the stereo behind the bar. Jason Keen held his Lady close, and they hobbled in slow circles around the dance floor. The kitchen staff came out to watch.

Mike felt his cover as dutiful and well-behaved son growing thinner by the minute. He decided not to wait for the promised anniversary cake. He wouldn't even ask to be excused. He dumped his napkin on the table and made for the exit, only to be ambushed as soon his sneakers hit the sand.

They came at him from all sides, their grins shining out of the dark. He toppled onto the sand as he was tackled, wrestling at least three at once. He tried to push them off, but there were too many. Samsam straddled him, pinning his arms to the sand. Two others held down his legs.

"Okay, okay," said Mike. "Uncle. I surrender."

A crowd of hyper children encircled them, jabbering excitedly in Malay. One of the boys hugged himself and made exaggerated kissing sounds as he sashayed around, mimicking the couple on the dance floor. The mob dissolved into giggles. Mike used the distraction to wriggle himself free, kicking sand at his attackers as he staggered to his feet.

The little ones came for him next. One jumped onto his shoulders for a piggyback ride, and Mike took off galloping around the beach, his little rider shrieking with joy.

"Hey buddy," said Mike over his shoulder. "You want to meet an old friend of mine?"

He slowed to a stop outside the cabin.

The little rider tightened his grip. "Go fast! Go fast!"

"You're gonna have to let go for a second," Mike said. "*Lepaskan.*"

The little boy loosened his strangling grasp and slid off Mike's back. He waited at the door, sucking on his finger, while Mike went inside. An electric light turned on, then went off again. When the American boy came back, he was clutching something orange and furry in his hand.

"What's your name?" said Mike, sitting down on the front steps. "*Siapa nama anda?*"

"Haruun."

"Well, Haruun, say hello to my old friend Charlie." He twitched the tiger's head to make it speak. "Nice to meet you. *Raahhrr.*"

Chapter 41

Mr. Keen had gone with the Lady of the Night to her cabin at the other end of the beach. Mike had the room all to himself. He wasn't used to sleeping alone, and the sounds kept him awake long into the night. The creak of wood as it cooled. The breeze shuffling through palm leaves. The monotonous whisper of waves against the shore.

Somehow things had got confused, and he didn't know who to believe anymore. Only that he had a promise to keep, and faith the size of a mustard seed. Faith enough to dream.

In the dream, he is playing basketball. He fakes out Austin and jumps high to score a perfect layup, just as the taxi comes chugging around the bend. Mom and Dad step out of the car into the gravel driveway. They are not in a particular hurry. He jogs across the concrete half-court to meet them, and Mom opens her arms wide. She doesn't care that he is sweaty, and she laughs as he hugs her. She smells slightly of lavender, her arms around him gentle and warm. Dad grins, reaching out a hand to ruffle his hair.

Where have you been? Mike asks. I was worried.

Oh, sweetheart, his mother says. We were kidnapped by the Vietcong. But everything's okay now. We're going to be together again.

Thanks to you, says Dad.

We're so proud of you, says Mom, hugging him. Then she tells him to get dressed, but her voice has changed. It is not his mother's voice at all. The scent of lavender is gone, replaced by a cheap and suffocating perfume.

Mike, I told you to get dressed, says the Lady of the Night. It's time to go.

The light was on. She had pulled the sheet off him, and his exposed body felt suddenly cold. He pulled the sheet back up to cover himself, blinking his eyes at the brazen light. The Lady loomed over his bed, wearing a track suit and running shoes. "Get moving," she said impatiently. "They'll be here any minute."

"Who?"

She grabbed his clothes off the chair and thrust them at him. "A boat is coming to pick us up."

"But it's the middle of the night," said Mike, tugging his shorts on. "Where's Mr. Keen?"

She didn't answer. She opened the cupboard door and looked inside. "Where is it?" she said. Her eyes hunted around the room until they settled on the duffel bag. She dragged it out from under the bed. "Is it in here?"

"Leave it alone!" Mike grabbed the shoulder strap and yanked hard, falling back onto the bed. He hugged the duffel against his chest. "I told you already. It's safe."

The Lady of the Night narrowed her eyes at him. "Don't play with me," she said. "Put your shoes on."

Mike was still fumbling with his laces when the Lady grabbed him by the wrist and hauled him out the door. He was surprised how strong she was. Her long nails dug into his wrist as she dragged him down the beach. The sky was just beginning to lighten across the sea. A speedboat waited at the end of the pier, gunning its engine.

"What about Mr. Keen?" he said.

She still hadn't let go of his arm. She squeezed tighter as she pulled. "Forget Keen. He's no concern of yours."

Something about the way she said it made him dig his heels into the sand. "What do you mean? Where is he? Is he okay?"

"You can't help him now," she said. "It's too late for that."

They had reached the foot of the pier. Two shadowy figures lurked at the other end, one in the boat, one on the dock. Mike glimpsed the barrel of a rifle, stark against the dawn sky.

She twisted his wrist until he winced. "Come on. We don't have time—"

He swept his arm counterclockwise, breaking out of her grasp.

"Mike!" she hissed. "Come get in the damn boat."

Mike shook his head, backing away, clutching the duffel bag close to his hip. "Something's wrong. Where's Mr. Keen?"

"He'll have to face the consequences sooner or later. He's a traitor, Mike."

"I don't care!"

"You little brat!" she said. "Get your butt in the boat!"

But he was already running. The bag flapping at his side, the sand slipping under his sneakers, the cabin leaning out of the dark. He took the front steps in a single leap and crashed through the door.

The bed was empty. Mike heard a moaning sound coming from somewhere. He flipped on the light switch next to the door. In the sudden garish light, a man was writhing on the floor.

"Mr. Keen!"

Mike dropped to his knees. Mr. Keen's face was twisted in pain. A thin trail of puke dribbled from the corner of his mouth. One hand clutched his stomach, and the other reached out helplessly. Mike didn't know what to do.

"Let him be," said the Lady of the Night.

Mike looked up and saw her framed in the doorway, the sea behind. "What did you do to him?"

"He ate some bad fish," she said. "He'll be fine."

"We all ate the same fish," said Mike.

The Lady lunged forward and yanked on the duffel bag, dragging Mike to his feet as she ripped it from his shoulder. "Last chance," she said.

"We can't leave him like this!"

The Lady shouldered the duffel and made a move to go, but stopped at the door to look back. "Too bad," she said. "You're cute, but you're a pain in the ass." Then she turned and ran.

For a second he watched her, sand flying from her heels, the duffel flapping at her side. Then he saw the men. Crouching on the sand, either side of the pier. A moment trapped inside its own eternity.

"Mike, get down!"

Mr. Keen pulled him to the floor and wrapped him in a fierce hug as the rat-tat-tat of machine-gun fire erupted from the beach. The walls splintered and sang.

Sometime later, the bone-crushing hold around his rib cage finally loosened. A speedboat engine whined, fading into the distance.

"Mr. Keen?"

The man had rolled onto his back. Blood was burbling between his lips, and his eyes looked scared. Mike knelt, slipped a hand under Mr. Keen's head and raised it gently off the floor but then didn't know what to do with it. He just held it.

"See any angels coming?" Mr. Keen sputtered between breaths.

"Shut up!" said Mike. "You're not going to die."

Mr. Keen laughed, then coughed, and turned his head away. Blood dribbled from his mouth onto the floor. "I see one," he said.

"No. No. No."

"I see an angel." Mr. Keen reached up with a bloody hand and grabbed Mike's shirt. His body curled into itself, his face crumpling in a spasm of pain. Someone pulled on Mike's shoulder, and he fell back against the bullet-splintered wall. The room was suddenly full of men in sarongs, shouting in Malay. They formed a huddle around the body on the floor, then lifted it in unison to shoulder height. Mr. Keen's bloody hand dangled as they carried him out the door and down the beach toward the launch.

People had come hurrying from the kampong, and a crowd of onlookers had gathered on the shore. Mike didn't feel anything. He walked down the beach, away from the crowd, thinking he might need to cry. But he didn't cry. Something was wrong with his eyes. He watched the launch as it chugged away from the dock, and he didn't feel anything at all.

Slowly he became aware that he was not alone. Barelegged children formed a quiet circle around him. Nobody was saying anything. He dropped to the sand, and a moment later he felt Samsam's arm around his shoulders.

A small boy pushed his way through the circle of knees. His little face was set in a solemn frown as he thrust the orange furry thing at Mike.

"Haruun," said Mike.

The little boy turned away and ran, leaving Mike clutching the tiger in both hands. He buried his face into its fur and wept.

Chapter 42

Name, rank, and serial number. That was all he was obliged to tell, according to the Geneva Convention. Except he didn't know what his rank was, he didn't have a serial number, and he wasn't really in a war.

He sat at a table in a small room with concrete walls and no windows. One wall had a mirror on it, and in the reflection he saw a boy with a dirty face and a bloody shirt and a scared look in his eyes.

He shifted in his chair and waited.

When they finally came, there were two of them. The first was a young police officer in uniform. The second was an older man wearing civilian clothes who sat on a chair in the back of the room. He was quiet and still like a sitting statue. Nothing in his face moved except his eyes.

The young officer flashed a friendly smile and waved at Mike as he entered, balancing a thick manila file and a portable tape recorder in one hand. "I'm Inspector Aidi," he said. "This is Superintendent Lo of Special Branch. We have a few questions, okay?"

Mike opened his mouth to answer, but only nodded. He seemed to have lost his voice somewhere.

Inspector Aidi inserted a cassette into the tape recorder and pressed a button. He checked his watch. "The time is 11:42. This is Inspector Aidi, Royal Malaysia Police. Also present is Special Branch Superintendent Lo. Interview is being conducted at Mersing Police Station, Johor." He smiled again at Mike. "Nothing to be scared about, okay? We're just trying to find out what happened. Let's start with your name, please."

Mike told him.

"So, Mike, perhaps you can explain…" Inspector Aidi opened the case file. He set a pair of passports on the table in front of Mike. "These were found in your father's possession. Why do you have two passports under two different names?"

Mike stared at the passports until they started to blur. One was a standard green U.S. passport. The other one was navy blue with a royal crest embossed on the cover.

"It's a simple question," said Inspector Aidi. "Are you Michael Turner of Oklahoma, USA? Or are you Michael Bennett of Ontario, Canada?"

Mike looked up. "Don't I get a lawyer or something?"

The brazenness of the question surprised even Mike. The young officer was caught off guard and glanced at the plainclothes man in the back. But the quiet superintendent sat stone still like a Buddha.

"Why?" said Aidi. "Do you feel you *need* a lawyer?"

"Maybe," said Mike.

The Inspector smiled and shook his head. "This isn't *Hawaii Five-0*, Mike. We do things differently here. Just answer our questions, and then you can go home."

Mike looked down at the table. "I don't know," he said.

"You don't know what?"

"I don't know where home is."

Aidi pulled out a chair and sat down. "Then let me help you. The Canadian Embassy knows nothing of a Michael Bennett from Ontario. Neither does Malaysian Immigration. The Canadian passport is a fake. A very *good* fake. As for the American one—"

"It's classified," Mike blurted. He immediately regretted it, but with the regret came a kind of relief. He had played his last card, and there was nothing else he could do now but wait.

The Inspector leaned back in his chair. "I beg your pardon?"

"I said it's *classified*," said Mike. "Top Secret."

"So, you think this is funny?"

"No, sir."

"What game are you playing?"

Mike kept his mouth shut, breathing hard through his nose as he looked the Inspector squarely in the eyes.

The Inspector stared back with a perplexed frown. "Entering the country with false documents is a serious crime. Don't you know how much trouble you're in?"

"Yes, sir," said Mike, thinking: *You have no idea.*

There was a movement in the back of the room. The quiet superintendent was standing up.

"Thank you, Inspector," he said, his face expressionless, his voice polite. "This has been most instructive. Special Branch will take it from here."

Chapter 43

The orders had come from above. Inspector Aidi was apologetic when he brought the news to Mike. "I've told them my strong objections," he said, "but Special Branch big shots are running things now. It's not standard procedure at all. But orders are orders."

Mike stood up from the bench in the holding cell. "So you're just going to turn me loose?"

"Within the hour," said Aidi. "I brought you some clean clothes." He squeezed a small Malaysian Airlines flight bag through the bars of the cage. "My nephew is about the same size as you. Also, there's a bus ticket, and your personal belongings."

Mike looked inside the bag and found Charlie the tiger snuggling peacefully under a faded Grateful Dead T-shirt.

"*Terima kasih*," said Mike.

"*Sama-sama*." They shook hands through the bars. "Before you go, Superintendent Lo would like a quiet word. Good luck, Mike."

The "quiet word" with Superintendent Lo took a little longer than expected. But by mid-morning Mike found himself on the sidewalk outside the police station, wearing a hand-me-down Grateful Dead T-shirt that was too big for him.

The sky was overcast, the street wet from a recent rain. A truck carrying a load of raw rubber rumbled past, spraying his legs with a fine mist of mud. Motor scooters buzzed in and out of the traffic. The damp air smelled like gasoline and overripe fruit.

Mike shouldered the flight bag and turned left toward the open-air market. He could sense he was being watched. Across the street, a man in a striped shirt was reading a newspaper outside the Chinese grocery. On the corner by the bank, a shoeshine boy looked too old for his trade and seemed more interested in Mike than in his customer's shoes.

Mike weaved his way among the market stalls. Some of the hawkers had spread their wares on straw mats on the ground. Old women with betel-stained teeth watched over piles of rice, dried peppers, spices. Shoppers haggled over pungent-smelling durians, plump ripe papayas, bundles of hairy rambutan. Skewers of chicken satay sizzled over hot coals. Fresh fish nestled half-buried under ice. A young man in a tie-dye shirt hawked pirated music tapes from atop an old wooden crate. "Grateful Dead," he said approvingly as Mike wandered past. "Special price for you, my friend."

The stalls began to thin out as he neared the bus station, the smells of market food mingling with diesel fumes. A bus had just turned into the depot when Mike caught sight of the black Cadillac. It was coming from the other direction, its interior darkened behind tinted windows. Mike watched as the boat-sized sedan cruised to a stop. The window on the driver's side cranked slowly down. A shadowy face said, "Well, if *you* aren't a sight for sore eyes."

Instinctively, Mike took a step back. He had never seen the colonel in civilian clothes before. Slacks and a batik shirt. Casual, like he was out for a weekend drive.

"Hop in, Mike," said the colonel. "Let's get you home."

Mike hesitated. "I'm supposed to take the bus," he said. "They gave me a ticket and everything."

The colonel affected a playful frown. "You think I'm going to let you take the bus, after everything you've been through?"

Some cars behind the Cadillac started honking.

"Get in the car, Mike," said the colonel. "You're holding up traffic."

Mike circled around the front of the car and got in on the passenger side. The plush interior of the car was cool and comfortable. As he shut the door, all the street sounds went suddenly quiet. The outside world, cut off, seemed only half real.

"Why didn't you pick me up at the police station?" Mike asked.

"Less paperwork this way," said the colonel, pulling out into the traffic. "No sense in tying ourselves up in red tape. How are you feeling?"

"Okay, I guess," said Mike. He didn't want to think about Mr. Keen right now.

The colonel seemed to read his thoughts. "It's a pity about Jason. In spite of how it ended, there was a time when he served his country well. That has to count for something."

Mike leaned his head against the window glass, peering into the side mirror as the colonel talked. The motor scooter that had been following two car-lengths behind suddenly peeled off onto a side street.

"I'm sorry you got caught up in all this, Mike," the colonel was saying. "It wasn't supposed to happen this way."

They passed a makeshift mosque on the edge of town. Shophouses gave way to rice paddies and rubber plantations. Lines of trees stood bleeding in a field, their milky wounds seeping into buckets.

"I know this is hard for you to understand, Mike, but sometimes right and wrong aren't as simple as they teach you in Sunday school. We're at war. Things get messy. "

Messy. The trail of vomit on the floor, the blood bubbling out of Mr. Keen's mouth, the lifeless hand dangling as they carried him out. Mike closed his eyes, but the image remained. He couldn't make it go away.

"It's about a four-hour drive to the border," said the colonel. "I thought we might stop off for a picnic lunch. How does that sound?"

"Okay."

"No point in hurrying," said the colonel. "It'll give us some time to catch up."

"Catch up?"

"I was thinking of a little information sharing. There are one or two things I'd like to clear up, if you don't mind."

"Like what?" said Mike.

The colonel didn't answer right away. He rested his elbow on the armrest and steered with one hand, as if settling in for a long drive. "Let's start with the police," he said. "What exactly did you tell them?"

"Just the truth," said Mike.

"The truth?" The colonel sounded doubtful. "And what truth was that?"

Mike shrugged. "That my martial arts teacher went crazy and kidnapped me. Isn't that what happened?"

"Okay," said the colonel. "What else?"

"They asked about the Lady. Who she was."

"And?"

"All I know is she's Mr. Keen's girlfriend. She just showed up. They spent the whole time making out. It was pretty gross, actually."

A trace of a smile dawned on the colonel's face. For a while they were quiet, and Mike watched the countryside whizzing past his window. A kampong surrounded by rice paddies. Women in straw hats stooping ankle-deep in the mud. A barelegged boy riding a water buffalo. Gradually the farmland faded into trees, and the jungle took over, closing in on them from both sides.

"You said information *sharing*," Mike said. "Does that mean I get to ask questions, too?"

"Fair's fair," said the colonel. He glanced in the rearview mirror and flicked the turn signal on. The car trundled off the main road onto a dirt track.

"Where are we going?" said Mike. "Is this the picnic place?"

"Almost there."

The car bounced over the rutted road, dense with trees on either side. After a few minutes they pulled over into a wide space and stopped.

"Would you mind grabbing the basket from the back?" said the colonel. He turned the engine off and took out the keys. Then he reached a hand under his seat to get something.

Mike stared. "What's the gun for?"

The colonel didn't look at Mike. He checked the safety on the Army-issue pistol before sliding it into a snug-fitting holster inside his shirt. "Just an overabundance of caution. You never know what you might run into out here. It's best to be prepared."

Mike nodded mutely. He started to open the passenger door but hesitated. "Where are we, anyway? Do we have to have our picnic so far from the road?"

The colonel smiled at him. "What's the matter, Mike? Not afraid of a little jungle hike, are you?"

Mike swallowed hard, thinking: *He knows. He knows everything I'm feeling. He knows what I'm thinking right now.* But he said, "No, sir," as he got out and waited for the colonel to open the trunk. Inside, a wicker basket with a closed lid sat next to the spare tire. It felt surprisingly heavy when he lifted it.

"Down that path, Mike," said the colonel. "Straight ahead. Can you manage?"

The path was hardly a path at all, more like an animal track of some kind. Tendrils like thin green fingers brushed his bare legs and arms and face. His skin broke out in sweat, trickling into the folds of his Grateful Dead T-shirt.

"Can I ask my question now?" Mike said. "Information sharing, you said. Fair's fair, right?" He didn't look back, but he could hear the colonel's footsteps and labored breathing behind him. "I just want to know what happened to my mom and dad, that's all. Where are they?"

No answer. Mike stumbled on. Weeds and creepers grew thick around his legs. "I get it, that it's need-to-know," he said. "But I really, *really* need to know."

The heavy picnic basket bumped against his knee. He thought he heard traffic up ahead, but it was only the sound of a rushing stream: a cascade of water glimmered through the tangle of leaves.

Mike stopped and turned around. "Sir?"

The colonel stood in the middle of the trail in a kind of trance, mournful and misty-eyed, gazing at Mike as if he were a ghost only half there. "She was going to betray us all," he said.

The picnic basket fell from Mike's hand and spilled its contents into the weeds. He bent down to scoop up what he had spilled, but there was nothing to pick up. Only rocks. The basket was full of rocks.

"She threatened to blow the whistle on everything," the colonel said, stepping closer. "All because of a weak, petty attack of conscience. You have to understand, Mike, we couldn't allow that to happen. There was too much at stake."

Mike took a step backwards, and then another. Creepers tickled the back of his neck. A large bird broke cover and flapped into the high trees. Behind him, the sound of rushing water grew louder.

The colonel stopped where the basket had tipped over. He squatted down among the weeds and chose a rock the size of a softball. He held it in one hand as he straightened up. His face had hardened.

"*Conscience*," he said, spitting the word out. "Of course, everyone has a right to follow their conscience. But when it threatens people's livelihoods, everything they've worked their whole lives to achieve—"

"You mean drug smuggling," said Mike.

The colonel sighed. "Congress would have cut off the flow of money in a heartbeat. It would have meant the end for Vietnam."

Tears scalded Mike's eyes. "Say what you did! Why won't you *say* it?"

"You can be proud of them, Mike. They made the ultimate sacrifice."

Mike took another step backwards but could go no further. He had backed into the mossy trunk of a tree. He stared at the rock in the colonel's hand. "So you're going to kill me too?" His voice sounded high and shrill above the rush of the stream.

"Do you believe in Heaven, Mike? It won't hurt. You will make it easier for both of us if you turn around."

"No!"

"It will be like you slipped while crossing the stream. Then everything will be beautiful and fine."

Mike had the feeling of being in the wrong movie. This should be the part where the police rush in to make their arrest, but nothing seemed to be happening according to script. Mike listened hard for the telltale sounds of voices and footsteps, but heard only jungle noises and the rushing of the stream. He couldn't wait any longer. The colonel's face had set in grim resolve, his fingers bloodless and white as they tightened around the rock.

"Oh, by the way," said Mike. He lifted the hem of his Grateful Dead T-shirt. Pulled it high up to his armpits, exposing his skinny chest and the clunky listening device taped to it. "Say hello to my friend Superintendent Lo," he said. "Royal Malaysia Police."

For a moment the colonel's lips formed a perfect 'O.' His eyes widened, and the rock fell from his hand. "Jesus Christ, you little—" He whipped the gun from its holster and turned, looking wildly around. The forest seemed to have gone quiet, except for the rippling of the stream. The colonel's gaze fell on Mike again, as if seeing him for the first time. A hardness crept into his eyes. "Did you really expect them to save you, Mike?" he said. "You have no *idea* what you're up against." He raised the pistol in a two-handed grip. "I'm sorry, Mike. I didn't want it to end this way, but—"

The colonel never finished his sentence. The boy's motion was so fluid, he hardly saw it at all. A loud *POP* exploded from the pistol as it flew from the colonel's hands. He stumbled backwards, and the boy moved in, delivering a rapid-fire series of punches and kicks. The trees began to tremble, and uniformed men sprang up out of the undergrowth. In seconds, the officers were upon them, shouting commands. But by that time the colonel was already flat on his back.

Chapter 44

Mike searched under his bed, hoping for a miracle, but all he found were the spider's dried-up remains. He laid Peter's body carefully in a matchbox and put him in his pocket. It had always been a far-fetched idea, that you could move mountains. But even if he didn't have faith the size of a mustard seed anymore, he still had the heart of a tiger. A very particular tiger with a very particular heart.

Bryan said, "*God*, Mike. Are you out of your mind?"

Krisda stared in disbelief. "You're taking him to school?"

Mike climbed into the van, carrying Charlie on top of his math book in plain sight. "Yeah, so?"

"The guy's got guts," said Krisda.

"The guy's suicidal," said Bryan.

But the girls thought it was cute. Some of them asked to pet his tiger. Saying how *brave* he was. Nobody dared tease him, since he had come back from the dead. He had been kidnapped by a drug-smuggling gang and escaped, if you believed the stories. Some said he had a black belt in Tae Kwon Do. There were rumors that he had almost killed a man.

Since his return, the weekly interrogation sessions with Miss Kumar had morphed into daily 'chats.' With time, he would start to feel normal again, she told him. Until then, every day after homeroom he had to go to Miss Kumar's office. Sometimes they talked about his mom and dad, the little ways in which they were still with him, how they came to him sometimes in dreams. Sometimes they talked about Mr. Keen. Most days the chat only lasted a few minutes, long enough to reassure her that he was okay.

* * *

Mike found him at their usual table in the cafeteria, shoveling noodles into his mouth with chopsticks while reading the latest *Green Lantern*.

Mike slid his tray onto the table and perched Charlie within licking distance of Jin Kim's *mee goreng*.

Jin Kim glanced at the tiger suspiciously.

"It's a present," said Mike. "Can you give it to your dad?"

Jin Kim screwed up his face. "Eh, that ugly thing?"

"He's not ugly, he's just old," said Mike. "Anyway, it's what's on the inside that counts. What's in his *heart*. Right?"

Jin Kim narrowed his eyes knowingly and gave a slight nod. He took Charlie and set him on the bench next to him. Then he flipped to the ads in the back of his comic and said, "Look, man. They got these sea monkeys now. Just add water. What you think, Mike?"

"It's a rip-off. Same as the X-ray glasses."

"*Wah piang* eh! Everything a rip-off now!"

"Listen," said Mike, "there's something I have to tell you. Something important."

"Old news," said Jin Kim, dipping his chopsticks into the bowl again. "I know about tiger already. Big scoop. Make my father number one reporter at *Straits Times*."

"Not that," said Mike. "Something else."

Jin Kim flicked a shrimp at Mike with his chopsticks. Mike unstuck it from his shirt and flicked it back.

"It's about Peter, my spider," said Mike. "He's dead."

Jin Kim's chopsticks stopped moving. Mike took the matchbox out of his pocket and laid it carefully on the table between them.

"Mike, sorry ah," said Jin Kim.

"No, you don't get it," said Mike. "I've been lying to you. He's been dead a long time."

Jin Kim shrugged. "Neh mind. We get other spider for you. World Championship go on, lah."

"No, you're not listening!" Mike clutched his head in his hands. "I lied to you the whole time. I stole your dad's notebook. And the most important thing you gave me, I killed."

There was a pause. Mike waited for the lightning bolt, the violent comeuppance that would end their impossible friendship. But instead Jin Kim said, "Mike, you blur like sotong! Spider not dead, only passed to next life. Come, let's go find him." Jin Kim gathered his bowl and chopsticks and prepared to bus his tray, while Mike stared.

"I told you, Peter's dead!"

Jin Kim looked at him curiously, his dark eyes shining, a smile half-formed on his lips. As if to say Mike was the one who hadn't been listening. Lunchtime noises were all around them: the murmur of voices like water over rocks, the sizzle and clatter of cooking in Mr. Ho's kitchen. From the playground, shrieks and laughter. Underneath it all, the beating of his own heart.

"Got matchbox," said Jin Kim. "Peter waiting. Can or not?"

Mike didn't know if it was the end of something or the beginning of something. But he was ready to find out.

"Can," he said.

Glossary

accuse me — excuse me

Alamak! — exclamation of surprise or amazement

also can (orso can) — That is also possible.

ang moh — a person of European descent (lit. "red beard")

auntie — an older lady (used as a term of respect)

ayam — chicken

bo cheng hu — in a state of anarchy or chaos

blur — confused

blur like sotong — confused like an octopus

borrow me — lend me

can — yes, it can be done

Can I hepch you? — Can I help you?

Can or not? — Is it possible?

Can you dun... — Please don't...

catch no ball — don't understand, or don't "get it"

chio bu — pretty girl

Don't play play. — Don't play around. Don't mess with.

Don't shy. — Don't be shy. Make yourself at home.

Early don't say. — Why didn't you say something before?

Engrish (Ingrish) — English

eksi — arrogant or full of oneself

fetch — drive or give a lift to someone

fly aeroplane — disappear from the scene, or abscond

havoc — busy, hectic, or hyper

how can? — how is it possible?

humtum — hit or strike a person

jude — pretty or sweet

joy — enjoy
kampong — a small village (Malay)
kayu — stupid
kiam pah — asking for trouble
lah — a syllable added to the end of a sentence for emphasis
lor — similar to 'lah' but with a less positive connotation
lai dat (liddat) — like that
lost form — endured an embarrassing situation
macam — like or similar to (used as a comparison)
makan — eat (Malay)
mee goreng — fried noodles
mm chai si — not afraid to die; no fear of the consequences
nasi goreng — fried rice (Malay)
neh mind (neh mine) — never mind
never see before? — So what?
no more already (orready) — out of stock
pai kia — bad boy, troublemaker
pai seh — forgive me
relak — relax
sabo — sabotage
sarong — a long piece of cloth worn wrapped around the waist
sayang — what a pity!
see first — wait and see how it goes
see no touch — Look, but don't touch.
shiok — exclamation of delight; delicious
sian — boring
solid siah! — great! awesome!
sotong — confused (lit. "octopus")
steady lah! — good going! (used as a compliment)
talk cock (tok cok) — talk nonsense
Very good, who ask you? — Serves you right.
wah! — wow!
wah liao! — super-wow!
wah piang eh! — What the hell!
What talking you? — What are you talking about?

www.ingramcontent.com/pod-product-compliance
Lightning Source LLC
Chambersburg PA
CBHW030319180626
46810CB00003B/1156

Acknowledgements

The Singapore of the 1970s is a place in time that no longer exists. As a non-Singaporean writer, I have had to rely on my own imperfect memory. But I also had some help from the following sources, which I can recommend to the reader.

For a better understanding of Singlish:

An Essential Guide to Singlish, by Miel Prudencio Ma. (Gartbooks, Singapore, 2003.)

Spiaking Singlish: A Companion to How Singaporeans Communicate, by Gwee Li Sui. (Marshall Cavendish International, 2017.)

For historical background on the 1970s heroin trade:

The Politics of Heroin in Southeast Asia, by Alfred W. McCoy. (Harper & Row, 1972.)

In addition, Tan Kok Yang's excellent memoir helped stir my own memories, and provided important context and detail:

From the Blue Windows: Recollections of a Life in Queenstown, Singapore, in the 1960s and 1970s, by Tan Kok Yang. (National University of Singapore, 2013.)

Terima kasih. — 谢谢 — Thank you lah.